Rosa, Sola

Rosa, Sola

Carmela A. Martino

CANDLEWICK PRESS
CAMBRIDGE, MASSACHUSETTS

First edition 2005

Library of Congress Cataloging-in-Publication Data

Martino, Carmela.
Rosa, sola / Carmela Martino. — 1st ed.
p. cm.
Summary: Longing for a sibling in 1966 Chicago, fourth-grader Rosa is delighted with her mother's pregnancy, until tragedy strikes and her family struggles to deal with its grief.
ISBN 0-7636-2395-4
[1. Grief — Fiction. 2. Family life — Illinois — Chicago — Fiction. 3. Only child — Fiction. 4. Italian Americans — Fiction. 5. Chicago (Ill.) — History — 20th century — Fiction.] I. Title.
PZ7.M3673Ro 2005
[Fic] — dc22   2004062875

2 4 6 8 10 9 7 5 3 1

Printed in the United States of America

This book was typeset in Giovanni Light and Centaur.

Candlewick Press
2067 Massachusetts Avenue
Cambridge, Massachusetts 02140

visit us at www.candlewick.com

In memory of my mother, Lina Arquilla,
and for Peter and Joseph Arquilla,
the brothers I never knew

✿

I

Owl Eyes

"CAN I HELP, Mrs. Morelli?" Rosa asked as her best friend's mother lifted baby Antonio from his crib. The baby kicked his chubby legs, beating the air with his bare feet. To Rosa's surprise, he wore only a T-shirt and diaper. She thought babies had to be bundled up all the time, even in summer.

Mrs. Morelli answered, "You can give me a *pannolino.*" She nodded at the stack of white cloths on the dresser, then laid the baby on her bed.

Rosa handed a diaper to Mrs. Morelli, who smiled and said, *"Grazie."*

"You're welcome." Rosa wanted to ask what else she could do, but a loud *clickety-clack* stopped her.

On the other side of the bed, AnnaMaria was shaking a lollipop-shaped toy over her brother's head. Antonio turned toward the sound.

"AnnaMaria," Mrs. Morelli said as she pulled off Antonio's plastic pants, "you should be as helpful as your friend."

"I help a lot, Mama." AnnaMaria dropped the noisy rattle onto the bed. "But changing diapers is yucky." She scrunched her nose and stepped back.

Rosa, however, drew closer. She watched, fascinated, while Mrs. Morelli undid Antonio's diaper pins and hooked them onto her apron strap.

"Did you have a good nap, *bambino mio?*" Mrs. Morelli said to the baby. Antonio smiled as if he understood. Rosa smiled, too.

When Mrs. Morelli cleaned his bottom,

though, the baby started crying. To distract him, AnnaMaria bent over and let her long brown hair dangle above his face. He stopped fussing and reached up.

"You can't catch it, silly," AnnaMaria said, turning her head from side to side. "I'm too fast for you."

Rosa thought, *It isn't fair.* AnnaMaria has a baby brother *and* two little sisters. Rosa didn't have anyone.

Before pinning on the new diaper, Mrs. Morelli took Antonio's tiny feet in one hand and rubbed baby powder over his bottom with the other. The powder's fragrance chased away the last of the dirty-diaper smell.

Finally, Mrs. Morelli pulled up Antonio's plastic pants. *"Finito."* She gave the baby's bottom a pat, then turned to Rosa. "You want to hold him while I wash my hands?"

"Can I?" Even though she was nine years old, Rosa had never held a baby.

"Of course." Mrs. Morelli pointed at a chair in the corner. "Sit down."

Rosa's heart pounded as she leaned forward in the chair.

Mrs. Morelli eased the baby into Rosa's arms, saying, "Just watch his head."

Rosa cradled the baby's bald head in her left elbow. He weighed more than she'd expected.

"AnnaMaria knows what to do if you need help," Mrs. Morelli said as she walked away.

Rosa feared Antonio might cry again after his mother left, but he didn't. Instead, he glanced around the room, his chocolate-colored eyes wide open. When he finally looked up at Rosa, she said, "Hello, Antonio." He stared right at her.

The pounding of Rosa's heart slowed as she stared back. Antonio's dark eyes seemed too big for his little, round face. Without looking up, Rosa said, "His eyes are huge."

"Yeah. I call them owl eyes," AnnaMaria said. "And watch this." AnnaMaria touched a finger to Antonio's palm. He immediately clenched his hand around it. She pulled away, but Antonio didn't let go. "He's really strong."

Rosa heard footsteps coming down the hall, then Luisa burst into the room. Luisa was the youngest of the three Morelli girls, and a real chatterbox for a three-year-old. "I can't find Dolly," she cried. "You said I could play with her. I want to make her talk."

"It's okay, Luisa," AnnaMaria said. "I'll help you find Dolly." AnnaMaria pried her finger from Antonio's grip. "I'll be right back, Rosa."

Rosa looked down at Antonio. Why would Luisa want to play with a plastic doll when she had a real live baby brother? He was better than any doll, even one that said "Mama" when you pulled its string. Antonio needed someone to take care of him. A doll didn't need anyone.

The baby blinked, fluttering his long, dark lashes. "Owl eyes," Rosa said out loud. Yes, the name fit.

She bent over and inhaled his baby-powder smell. Too bad her hair was tied back, not loose like AnnaMaria's so that Antonio could play with it.

Rosa reached her right hand up from under the baby and touched her pinkie to his palm. He wrapped his hand around her finger, as he had done to AnnaMaria. A warm, tingly feeling spread through Rosa's whole body.

She pressed her face against his. His cheek felt softer than the angora scarf Ma had knitted her for Christmas. "Oh, Antonio," Rosa whispered. "I wish you were *my* brother."

Mrs. Morelli returned before AnnaMaria did. "I'm sorry, Rosa." She took the baby from Rosa. "AnnaMaria should not have left you *sola.*"

"But I wasn't alone." Rosa smiled up at Mrs. Morelli. "Antonio was with me."

Rosa didn't feel alone until she had to walk home by herself. *Sola.* Just thinking the word made her lonely. With Papa at work, Ma would be the only one home. And she'd be busy sewing for her customers.

Rosa reached into her pocket for the baseball Uncle Sal had caught at Wrigley Field the day before. Every June, her great-uncle took her to a Cubs game to celebrate the start of summer, but this was the first time he'd caught a foul ball there. A real major-league baseball. The ball's stitching felt bumpy under Rosa's fingers.

Showing the ball to AnnaMaria had been Rosa's excuse to visit her friend. Ever since Antonio had been born, Ma had kept Rosa from going to the Morellis' — she didn't want Rosa to be a bother. Now Rosa couldn't wait to tell Ma how she hadn't been a bother, but a help, and how Mrs. Morelli had let her hold the baby.

As Rosa skipped home, she tossed the ball into the air. It came down faster than she expected and landed with a thump alongside the Kowalskis' back fence. The ball just missed a pair of girl's red-and-white polka-dotted shorts hanging at the end of the crowded clothesline. Rosa recognized the shorts. They belonged to Debbie, the next-to-youngest of the six Kowalski kids. Debbie had been in Rosa's third-grade class.

Most of the kids at Our Lady of Mercy School came from big families like the Kowalskis. Debbie often teased Rosa about being the only one in their class without a brother or sister. Rosa didn't know which she hated more — being lonely or being different.

One thing she did know — she wanted a baby brother.

She picked up the baseball and tucked it into her pocket.

When Rosa reached home, her Sunday dress was the only thing on the backyard clothesline. As she watched the pink flowered dress fluttering all alone in the wind, the idea came to her. At Mass next Sunday, she would say an extra-special prayer. She would ask God to send her a baby brother. One just like Antonio.

2

Heartfelt Prayers

THREE WEEKS LATER, Papa drove Ma and Rosa to Fullerton Avenue Beach to celebrate the Fourth of July. As they crept along in the holiday traffic, Rosa shifted from side to side to keep her legs from sticking to the vinyl seat. She could hardly wait to get to the beach. Swimming with Papa was a special treat. During the busy summer construction season, Papa's bricklaying job left little time for fun.

Papa parked the car and they found a spot on the crowded beach. *"Andiamo,* Rosa," Papa said as soon as they were settled. "Let's see how the water is." Rosa left Ma sitting on their blanket and followed him.

When Rosa stepped into Lake Michigan, her skin broke out in goose bumps. "It's freezing!"

"Here, I'll help you get used to it," Papa said. He bent down and splashed her with both hands.

Rosa shrieked, then splashed him back.

Papa laughed. "Catch me if you can!" He dove into the water.

Rosa plunged in after him.

They had their own special rules for water tag: Papa never went in the really deep water. He always swam slow enough for Rosa to catch him. And when Papa was "it," he counted to ten before chasing Rosa.

Despite the cold water, Rosa soon caught up to Papa. "Gotcha," she said, tagging his leg. But as she started to swim away, someone called, "Look out!"

A black Frisbee came flying right at Rosa.

Before she could react, Papa lunged forward and blocked it from hitting her in the face.

He snatched the Frisbee, then turned to yell at the boy who had hollered the warning. "What's the matter with you!" Papa stood up, stretching to his full height. He was only five foot ten, but his thick muscles made him seem taller. As he scowled at the boy, Papa's heavy eyebrows joined to form one dark hairy line across his forehead. Rosa shivered. That look meant trouble.

Papa shook the Frisbee at the boy. "You trying to kill somebody?"

"I'm really sorry, Mister," the boy said. "I was throwing to *him*." He motioned toward another boy standing about six feet to Rosa's right. The other boy waved, then swam for shore.

Papa clutched the Frisbee, still scowling. Rosa reached up and squeezed his outstretched arm. "It was an accident, Papa."

Papa lowered his arm. He put his free hand on Rosa's shoulder. "You okay, Rosalina?"

Rosa nodded. "The Frisbee didn't even touch me."

"All right then." Papa turned to the boy. "Next time, you be more careful." Papa tossed the Frisbee back. As he watched the boy swim away, Papa's eyebrows returned to normal.

Relieved, Rosa scooped a handful of water and splashed him. "You're it, remember?"

"Oh, I forgot." He ruffled her hair, then began counting, "*Uno, due, tre . . .*"

Rosa swam off, happy to return to their game. They played water tag till her arms and legs ached. Then Rosa headed toward the beach while Papa went for a swim in the deep water.

Halfway back to shore, she stopped to scan the beach for Ma. A little boy wearing a white sailor hat caught Rosa's attention. He stood at the edge of the water, clutching the handle of a green bucket. He looked afraid to step into the lake. Then a girl about Rosa's age came up alongside him. She took the boy's free hand and led him into the water. She stomped her foot, splashing the boy's legs. The boy laughed and stomped his foot too, splashing himself as much as his sister. Rosa smiled. But she couldn't help wondering, When would *she* have a little brother to play with?

Rosa finally spotted Ma in her yellow sundress—Ma couldn't swim, so she didn't even own a swimsuit. Rosa waved, and Ma waved back. The day before had been the third Sunday Rosa had prayed for a baby brother at Mass, but she still didn't see any change in Ma. Why was God taking so long to answer her prayers?

Suddenly, Rosa felt two strong hands gripping her waist. She turned just as Papa lifted her out of the water. "Hey," she cried, pounding his wet shoulders. "Put me down, you big sea monster."

"If you say so," he said, tossing her into the lake.

She jumped up and ran for shore with Papa only steps behind.

When she reached their blanket, Ma handed her a towel. "How's the water?"

Rosa shivered and wrapped the towel around herself. "Cold!"

"Here, Frannie, feel for yourself." Papa bent over and shook his head toward Ma. Water sprayed everywhere.

Ma raised her arms. "*Basta*, Joe!" she said, laughing. "Enough!"

Papa kissed Ma's cheek, dripping water onto the shoulder of her sundress. He dabbed the wet spot with his towel. "There, all better."

Ma laughed again. Rosa smiled. Her mother's laughter always reminded her of a bird chirping.

"Off with you," Ma said, pushing Papa away. "Before you soak the blanket."

Papa spread his towel on the closest patch of bare sand and lay down on his back. The beads of water clinging to the hair on his chest glistened in the sun. Rosa wished she could have more days like this with Papa. But he worked six days a week, from early in the morning till almost dark. Except for holidays, Sunday was Papa's only day off—his day to catch up on sleep and chores. He didn't even go to Mass with Rosa and Ma unless it was a special occasion.

Ma had just finished combing the tangles from Rosa's wet hair when a high-pitched cry filled the air. Rosa turned to see a little girl rubbing her eyes, her face partially hidden by her long blond hair.

"Mommy," the girl cried between sobs. "I want Mommy."

Several people gathered around her on the ledge that separated the beach from the park. A tall woman wearing horn-rimmed glasses stared down at the girl and said, "Are you lost, honey?"

"What's your name?" asked an old man with a cigar.

A teenager wearing a tie-dyed shirt held out a bag of potato chips. "You hungry, kid?"

The girl cried even louder, "Mommy!"

Rosa felt sorry for the little girl. How would she ever find her mother in such a crowd? Before Rosa could say anything, Ma got up. Rosa followed.

Ma sat down on the ledge next to the girl so they were eye to eye. "What a pretty bathing suit," Ma said. "Are those fishies?"

The girl sniffled, then nodded.

"So many bright colors. Do you know what color this is?"

The girl looked down at the fish Ma pointed at. "Orange."

"That's right. And this one?"

"Green," the girl answered.

"Yes. Now, tell me, can you remember what color bathing suit your mama is wearing today?"

The girl nodded. "Blue and white." She wiped the tears from her cheeks.

"Very good." Ma pointed at herself. "My name is Francesca. And this is my daughter, Rosa." Ma touched Rosa's arm, her hand warm

16

against Rosa's skin. "We want to help you find your mama. If I pick you up, you will see better. Okay?"

"Okay."

"Your hair is so beautiful," Ma said as she lifted the girl. "Is your mama's the same color?"

The girl nodded.

Ma soon had her talking in sentences. The girl told Ma her name was Patty, she was three years old, and she had a dog named Buster. When her daddy went to buy some hot dogs, Buster ran off after a squirrel. Patty tried to catch him and got lost.

Poor little Patty. Ma would never have let Rosa wander off like that.

Rosa followed Ma and Patty across the blanket-covered beach. The hot sand scorched the bottom of Rosa's feet, and before long her head ached from searching the crowd. She didn't see any blond woman in a blue-and-white swimsuit. Maybe Patty was wrong. After all, she was only three.

As they trudged on, the Beach Boys' "Wouldn't It Be Nice" blared from someone's transistor radio. Patty leaned her head against Ma's, her hair bright yellow next to Ma's dark curls. Rosa wondered what it would be like to brush that long blond hair. Maybe if they didn't find her mother, Patty could move in with Rosa's family. Rosa really wanted a baby brother like Antonio, but a little sister would be fun, too. Rosa began singing in her mind, "Wouldn't it be nice to have a brother and a sister . . ."

"Where's Mommy?" Patty asked Ma. Her voice sounded so sad, Rosa felt sorry for what she'd been thinking.

"Don't worry," Ma said. "We will find her."

They had almost reached the bathhouse when Rosa spotted a blond woman talking to a policeman. The woman was wearing a white beach cover-up over a navy blue swimsuit. She stood with her back to them, waving frantically toward the park.

Rosa pointed. "Over there, Patty. Is that your mother?"

"Mommy!" Ma set Patty down and she ran toward the woman.

The woman turned around. "Patty!" She scooped up Patty, hugging her tight. "Where did you go? I was so worried."

"I got lost, Mommy. They helped me find you." Patty pointed at Rosa and Ma.

"Thank you so much!" Patty's mother pressed her daughter's cheek against her own tear-streaked face. Their matching yellow hair looked like a halo holding their heads together. "How can I ever repay you?"

"No need," Ma said. She put her arm around Rosa. "I know what it is to have a daughter."

The words made Rosa's heart swell. She leaned her head on Ma's shoulder. Ma tilted her own head against Rosa's and gave her a sideways hug. Rosa wondered if they had a halo, too.

Back on the blanket, Rosa said, "You were so good with Patty, Ma. How did you do that?"

Ma shrugged. "I like children, that's all."

"Then why didn't you have more after me?"

"I wanted to, Rosa." Ma put her hand on Rosa's. "But they never came."

"Why not?"

Ma hesitated, then said quietly, "I guess you are old enough to know now. Something happened to me when you were born. I am a small woman and you were a big baby." Ma touched her belly with her free hand. "The doctor said it would be hard for me to ever carry a baby inside again."

A queasy feeling crept into Rosa's stomach. She pulled her hand from Ma's. "Then it's *my* fault?"

"No, no, *cara.*" Ma brushed a strand of hair from Rosa's forehead. "Do not blame yourself. It is no one's fault. In the Old Country we call it *destino.* Destiny. It was not meant to be."

"Then I've been praying for something impossible?"

"You have been praying I should have a baby?"

Rosa nodded. "A baby boy, just like Anna-Maria's brother." After what Ma had just said, though, it sounded pretty foolish.

"The doctor never said it is *impossibile*, Rosa. Only that there is not much chance." Ma put her finger under Rosa's chin and lifted her face. "Nothing is *impossibile* for God."

"Really?" Rosa felt hopeful again. "So it's okay to keep praying?"

"Of course it's okay." Ma hugged Rosa. Then she pointed at Papa, asleep on his towel. "You better wake your papa now, before the sun turns him into a lobster."

On the way home in the car, Rosa thought of what Ma had said about destiny. But Ma's words hadn't calmed the queasiness in Rosa's stomach. *She* was the reason Ma hadn't had more kids.

Rosa closed her eyes. Maybe if she prayed for forgiveness, God would make everything all right. She reached for the gold cross she always wore around her neck. Holding the cross, she prayed in her mind. "Dear God, I'm really sorry I hurt Ma when I was born. Please forgive me, and fix it so she can have a baby again." Then Rosa recited the Act of Contrition.

She let go of the cross and opened her eyes. What should she do for her penance? The hardest penance Monsignor Kelly had ever given her was to pray a decade of the rosary — ten Hail Marys — just for talking back to Ma. Rosa decided to give herself the toughest penance she could think of: a whole rosary.

The car stopped at a red light. Through the open window, Rosa saw a woman pushing a blue baby buggy. She wondered if the baby inside was a boy, like Antonio.

Rosa got another idea. Instead of praying for a baby brother once a week at Mass, she would say a rosary every day. And she wouldn't stop till Ma was pregnant. Then God would *have* to answer her prayers. "God always answers heartfelt prayers," Sister Mary Giles had told Rosa's third-grade class, "as long as they're for something that will bring you good." Rosa couldn't imagine how Ma having a baby could bring anything but good.

3 ✿

White Butterfly

FROM THAT DAY on, Rosa prayed the rosary every night. She said the five decades of Hail Marys sitting up in bed so she wouldn't fall asleep. She didn't tell her mother, though. Ma wouldn't like Rosa staying up past her bedtime, even if it was to pray.

And every morning Rosa checked to see if Ma's belly had grown at all. But the weeks passed without any change. By the time September arrived, Ma actually looked thinner. Rosa began to worry she was doing something wrong. What other reason could there be for God not answering her prayers?

On Labor Day, Rosa's family went to Uncle Sal's for a barbecue. They found Uncle Sal in the backyard, flipping sausages on the grill.

"*Ciao,*" Uncle Sal said, waving hello. Rings of sweat had already soaked the armpits of his red-and-green Hawaiian shirt.

"You are working?" Papa said as he shook his uncle's free hand. "On a holiday?"

"Eh!" Uncle Sal pushed back his straw hat. "When you are retired, every day is a holiday."

Ma kissed Uncle Sal's cheek and pointed at the sausages. "The *salsiccie* smell wonderful, Uncle Sal."

"I made them last night." Uncle Sal put the cover on the grill. "Wait till you taste." He brought the fingers of his right hand together and kissed them.

He turned to Rosa. "And how's my favorite goddaughter?"

Rosa grinned. As far as she knew, she was his *only* goddaughter. "Fine."

Uncle Sal kissed Rosa on both cheeks. "What's this?" He reached behind her left ear and pulled out a shiny quarter. "Forget to wash behind your ears?" Rosa giggled. Uncle Sal always had a trick or joke for her. And he even let her keep the quarter.

"Buon giorno," Aunt Ida called as she slid open the patio door. "It is a beautiful day, no?"

Aunt Ida greeted Ma and Papa, then turned to Rosa. "Hello, child." She bent to kiss Rosa, but her ruby-painted lips never touched Rosa's cheeks. Aunt Ida gave only pretend kisses. It was a good thing, too. Any closer and Rosa might have passed out from the smell of her perfume.

"All ready to go back to school, Rosa?"

Rosa shrugged. Her godmother was nothing like Uncle Sal. His straw hat covered a bald head surrounded by a ring of gray hair. Aunt Ida had thick, dark brown hair she wore in a tight bun at the back of her neck. Rosa didn't know if it was Aunt Ida's hair or her long, pointy nose, but she reminded Rosa of the lady in *The Wizard of Oz* who tries to take Toto away.

"Sit down, everyone," Aunt Ida said, pointing at the black iron patio chairs. "Claudia isn't coming. She's at her brother-in-law's today. So we can eat as soon as the *salsiccie* are done."

Aunt Claudia was Papa's sister. She and Uncle Mario had two sons close to Rosa's age. Rosa slumped in her chair. The day would be boring without her cousins to play with.

The afternoon was warm, but a gentle breeze cooled them as they ate in the shade of the patio umbrella. Uncle Sal's sausages *were* delicious. And Aunt Ida had prepared roasted red peppers, tomato-cucumber salad, and warm green beans in olive oil — all vegetables from Uncle Sal's garden. Rosa ate till her stomach couldn't hold anymore. Then she leaned back in her chair, her eyes half-closed.

Papa raised his glass for a toast. "To our

hosts," he said, pointing his glass of wine toward Uncle Sal and Aunt Ida. "For providing such a wonderful feast. *Salute!*"

As the adults clinked their glasses, Rosa stretched and tried to shake off her sleepiness.

Papa set his empty glass on the table. "I have some news," he said. Ma put her hand on Papa's, but he waved it off. Before Rosa could figure out what was going on, Papa blurted out, "Frannie is *incinta.*"

Rosa jumped up so fast her chair fell over with a loud clang. Had she heard right? Did Papa really say Ma was going to have a baby?

"Well, well," Uncle Sal said. He stood and shook Papa's hand. *"Congratulazioni,* Giuseppe." Uncle Sal tipped his hat to Ma. "Francesca."

"Yippee!" Rosa yelled. She *had* heard correctly. God had finally answered her prayers.

Rosa righted the overturned chair, then skipped around the table. The first time around, she hugged Ma. The second time, Papa. Then Uncle Sal. After four times around the patio, she even hugged Aunt Ida. Rosa wasn't going to be an only child anymore!

When she stopped to catch her breath, Rosa noticed Ma frowning at Papa. Was she angry with him for sharing the good news?

Uncle Sal poured wine into everyone's glasses, including Rosa's. "Another toast," he said. *"Mille auguri!"* He held his glass high. "Best wishes for a healthy baby."

Rosa clinked her glass against everyone else's. The sunlight shining through the glass made the red wine look like a sparkling jewel. But when Rosa took a sip, the wine burned her throat. It left a bitter taste in her mouth.

"This is cause for celebration," Uncle Sal said. "Let me see if I have any cigars." He waved for Papa to follow him.

After the men went inside, Aunt Ida said, "This is a big *sorpresa.*"

"It's a surprise for us, too." Ma's frown faded. "That's why I asked Joe not to say anything yet. But he's so excited. He's counting on a son this time."

Aunt Ida started scraping bits of food from Uncle Sal's plate onto hers. She said in Italian, "I don't think this is such a good idea, Francesca."

A little white butterfly fluttered by, and Rosa followed it over to Uncle Sal's garden. She never spoke Italian anymore, so Aunt Ida probably didn't realize Rosa understood her. Still, Rosa didn't want her godmother to suspect she was listening.

"I mean," Aunt Ida went on, "isn't it a bit risky to be pregnant at your age? You didn't have it too easy the first time."

Risky? Rosa held her breath and waited for Ma's answer. The butterfly hovered over Uncle Sal's pepper plants.

"Nonsense," Ma said, speaking Italian, too. "My mother was forty-two when she had her youngest. I'm only thirty-seven."

Rosa let go of the breath she'd been holding. The butterfly flew up into one of Uncle Sal's apple trees.

"When is the baby due?" Aunt Ida asked.

"April twenty-eighth," Ma said. "The day before Rosa's birthday."

Rosa hugged herself. What a wonderful birthday present!

Aunt Ida said to Ma, "By then you'll be thirty-eight."

Ma's lilting laugh eased Rosa's fears. "Aunt Ida, you worry because you've never had children yourself," Ma said. "My mother gave birth seven times without any trouble. I'm sure everything will be fine."

The butterfly sailed up over the apple tree. Rosa watched till it was a tiny speck against the blue sky, then closed her eyes. Spreading out her arms, Rosa imagined she was that little white butterfly, fluttering up to heaven. When she got there, she'd whisper in God's ear, "Thank you, God, for answering my prayer."

4 ❧

Noisy Flock

MA WASHED DISHES and Rosa dried while Aunt Ida put away the cookout leftovers. In her excitement, Rosa worked quickly.

"That was fast," Aunt Ida said when they had finished. "*Mille grazie.* Now, you two go back outside while I make coffee."

In the backyard, Papa and Uncle Sal were playing checkers at the table, so Ma sat on the metal gliding bench at the edge of the patio. She patted the spot next to her. "Come, Rosa."

Rosa sat down on the pale blue bench. The seat felt warm against her legs. She pushed off with her feet and the glider creaked into motion.

"Please don't." Ma put down her feet to stop the glider. "My stomach, it is not so good these days." She placed a hand on her belly. "That is why I went to the doctor. I thought I was sick."

"When did you see the doctor?"

"Last Tuesday, when you were at Anna-Maria's," Ma answered. "I didn't want you to worry, so I asked Signora Morelli to invite you over."

"Does Mrs. Morelli know about the baby?"

Ma nodded. "I told her Saturday, after the doctor called to say the test was positive. But I asked her not to say anything to AnnaMaria till after I told you." Ma put her hand on Rosa's shoulder. "I'm sorry, Rosa."

"Sorry? For what?"

"For not telling you about the baby sooner." Ma shook her head. "I can hardly believe it myself."

"It sure took God a long time to answer my prayers."

Ma's eyes widened. "You were still praying for a brother?"

Rosa nodded.

"After all this time," Ma said, "I thought you would have given up."

Rosa sat up tall. "I prayed a rosary every night since the Fourth of July."

"Oh, Rosa." Ma hugged Rosa, whispering in her ear, "You are an angel!"

The bench creaked, but didn't move. Even so, Rosa felt as though she were flying.

Wednesday morning, Rosa and Ma met up with AnnaMaria and her family on the way to school. "What a cute hat," Rosa said when she saw Antonio sitting in his stroller. She bent over and stroked the top of his navy blue cap. "I didn't know they made baseball caps that little." Antonio looked up at her with his big owl eyes and smiled. Rosa felt as though someone had tied a string around her heart and Antonio was tugging on it. She longed to hold him again, the way she had that first time. With April seven months away, it would be a long time before she could hold her own baby brother or sister.

"Come on," AnnaMaria said, pulling at Rosa's jumper. "We don't want to be late the first day."

As they hurried along, AnnaMaria's sister Caterina skipped beside them, her pigtails bouncing up and down. Ma fell in behind the three girls and talked with Mrs. Morelli, who was helping Luisa push the stroller.

AnnaMaria asked Rosa, "Are you happy about your mom having a baby?"

Rosa nodded. "I can't wait to see Debbie Kowalski's face when I tell her. Now she can't tease me about being an only child anymore."

"Rosa," Caterina interrupted, "today is my first day of kindergarten."

"It is?" Rosa tried to sound surprised. "You

look so big in your uniform, I thought you were a first grader."

Caterina beamed. "I'm in room twelve." She held out her Flintstones pencil case, labeled with her name and a large black number twelve.

"Do you know your teacher's name?" Rosa asked.

Caterina nodded. "Miss Leslie."

"Miss Leslie? Is she new?"

"Yeah," AnnaMaria answered. "Old Pruneface finally retired. I bet she was a hundred years old."

Patrick O'Shea had given their kindergarten teacher the nickname. But Rosa had always been too afraid of Sister Mary Thaddeus to call her that, even behind her back.

"A new teacher—you're so lucky, Caterina," Rosa said. "I'm sure Miss Leslie will be really nice."

"AnnaMaria," Caterina said, "tell me again about kindergarten."

As AnnaMaria described the basement classroom to Caterina, Rosa thought of her own first day at Our Lady of Mercy. Four years had passed since that September morning in 1962, but the memory was still vivid. Rosa's family had just moved into the neighborhood, and she felt frightened surrounded by so many strangers in a strange classroom. She tried to keep Ma from leaving.

"*Non mi lasciare,*" Rosa pleaded.

Ma hugged Rosa goodbye. "*Coraggio, cara.*"

Rosa tried to be brave. As Ma backed away, Rosa called, "*Ciao.*" But after her mother left, Rosa started crying.

A boy called out, "Look at the crybaby!"

Rosa froze. The room was suddenly quiet. Rosa felt everyone's eyes on her. She didn't know what to do. Sister Thaddeus was out in the hall.

The boy came closer. "What's the matter, crybaby?" he said. "Can't you talk English?"

Rosa wiped her face with the back of her hand. "I am *not* a crybaby," she said. "And I can talk just fine."

"Then why'd you say those funny words to your mother?"

Funny words? What did he mean? She'd learned to speak Italian first, before English. Did that make her strange?

Before Rosa could think of something to say, a girl behind her answered the boy. "Because she knows *two* languages — English and Italian." The girl put her arm around Rosa's shoulder. "How many languages do *you* know, Patrick?"

Patrick marched off without answering.

"*Ciao*," the girl called after him. "That's goodbye."

"But *ciao* can mean hello, too," Rosa added, then covered her mouth and giggled.

The other girl giggled, too. "My name's AnnaMaria Morelli," she said to Rosa. "What's yours?"

Now, as they neared school, Rosa glanced at AnnaMaria, who was still explaining kindergarten to Caterina. "The best thing about school," AnnaMaria told her sister, "is all the new friends you'll make." AnnaMaria smiled at Rosa.

Rosa smiled back. She and AnnaMaria had been friends ever since that first day of kindergarten. But that was also the day Rosa stopped talking Italian, even at home. She didn't like feeling strange.

At school, AnnaMaria and Rosa said goodbye to their mothers, then joined the other fourth graders. "Hey, everybody," AnnaMaria said. "Rosa has some news!"

Rosa looked right at Debbie Kowalski. "My mom's having a baby."

Debbie's mouth fell open. For once, she didn't have anything to say.

The other girls did, though. They all started talking at the same time.

Lynn Anderson said, "Oh, Rosa! You're so lucky!"

"When's your mom due?" Bridget Sullivan asked.

The sound of loud honking suddenly

drowned out their voices. Rosa looked up to see a group of geese flying in a large V across the sky.

Bridget tugged on Rosa's shirtsleeve. "Never mind the geese. Are you going to have to share your room with the baby?"

Rosa turned back to the girls gathered around her and smiled, happy to finally be part of the flock.

5 ❧

Christmas Eve

THE REST OF September and all through October, Rosa watched to see if Ma gained weight. But Ma's morning sickness lasted a long time. She didn't really start to look pregnant till the middle of December.

Rosa watched, too, to see if Ma slowed down at all. She didn't. In between her sewing jobs and household chores, Ma worked on crocheting a new coverlet for Rosa's bed.

After Christmas break began, Ma kept Rosa too busy to think much about the baby.

Thanksgiving had been at Aunt Claudia's house, so Christmas Eve was Ma's turn to have everyone over. Rosa spent the first week of her vacation helping Ma with the holiday baking, cleaning, and decorating.

Christmas Eve, Papa's sister's family arrived first. Aunt Claudia walked in the front door wearing a brown fake fur coat that made her look like a giant teddy bear. *"Buon Natale!"* she said, wrapping her teddy bear arms around Ma. Aunt Claudia was only three inches taller than Ma, but twice as wide. "I'm glad you're finally showing, Frannie." She patted Ma's belly and they both laughed.

Aunt Claudia hugged Rosa next. Even in December, Aunt Claudia smelled of lily of the valley, Rosa's favorite flower. Unlike Aunt Ida, Aunt Claudia gave real kisses. Aunt Claudia kissed Rosa on both cheeks, then stepped back and said, "How can you have grown so much since Thanksgiving?" Rosa smiled.

"You better watch out, Primo," Aunt

Claudia said to her son, who was six months older than Rosa. "Rosa will soon pass you up."

Primo stood up straighter. "No she won't. I'm growing too."

"Me, too," said his six-year-old brother, Enzo. Then Enzo wrinkled his nose. "What's that smell?"

"It's fish, of course," Primo said, trying to sound grown-up. "Did you forget? We never eat meat on Christmas Eve."

Enzo started to say, "I don't like—" but Uncle Mario said, "Shh," and bent down to unbutton Enzo's heavy winter coat. If Aunt Claudia was a teddy bear, Uncle Mario was a giraffe: tall, thin, and quiet. Rosa took the coats from him and carried them to Ma's room, just off the dining room.

When Uncle Sal and Aunt Ida arrived, everyone gathered around the dining-room table for their traditional Christmas Eve dinner, which included pasta with *calamari* sauce, poached *baccalà,* and baked *anguilla.* Rosa didn't like baked eel, but Aunt Ida insisted she eat at least a tiny piece *"per devozione."* Aunt Ida always found a way to spoil things.

After dinner, Rosa sat on the living-room floor playing Sorry! with her cousins while Papa, Uncle Sal, Uncle Mario, and Aunt Claudia played cards at the dining-room table. Ma and Aunt Ida were in Rosa's bedroom, next to the kitchen, looking at the new coverlet Ma had crocheted.

Primo easily won the first game of Sorry! He was reshuffling the game cards when Uncle Sal said to Papa, "Giuseppe, I received a letter from my brother Pasquale last week. You know, he is counting on the baby being a boy."

When she heard the word "baby," Rosa stood and walked over to the table.

"Certo," Papa said to Uncle Sal. "Then my father could go to his grave in peace—there would finally be someone to carry on the Bernardi name."

Rosa hadn't thought of that when she'd

prayed for a brother. She knew that Papa's older brother had died in World War II, leaving Papa with three younger sisters. But since most of Papa's relatives lived in Italy, Rosa didn't think about them very much. Now she realized that her father was the only one who could give Nonno Pasquale a grandson with the family name.

"I got a letter, too," Aunt Claudia said as she placed a card face-up on the table. They were using the Italian playing cards, and her card had three gold-colored coins on it. "If Frannie has a boy, Pa plans to change his will so that the baby gets the olive grove." Aunt Claudia shook her head. *"Non è giusto."*

"Of course it's fair," Papa said, throwing down a five of swords. He sat up taller. "The *maschio* who keeps alive the Bernardi name deserves as much."

"What about the other grandchildren?" Aunt Claudia said. "They'll each end up with a small share of a crumbling-down house while the baby inherits the only *proprietà* worth any-thing." She nodded at Uncle Mario, who placed a two of cups on the table without say-ing a word. Rosa moved in closer.

Aunt Claudia put a hand on Rosa's arm. "Why should Rosa's brother be entitled to more than her just for being born a boy?"

"This is a matter of *onore*, not money." The tone of Papa's voice made Rosa cringe. She tried to think of a way to change the subject. Aunt Claudia could be as quick-tempered as Papa. Their discussions sometimes turned into terrible arguments.

"Besides," Rosa's father went on, "this is Pa's decision to make. It's his will."

Uncle Sal said quietly, "*Sì*, it is Pasquale's will." Uncle Sal seemed sorry he'd mentioned Nonno's letter. He stared at his cards for a moment, then said, "Ah, a point for Giuseppe and me." He put down a king and picked up all the cards that had been played.

Aunt Claudia let go of Rosa. "Well, I'm going to write to Pa." She laid the rest of her cards on the table. "And tell him he should leave his will the way it is."

Papa threw down his remaining cards. The king of swords flew across the table and landed at Rosa's feet. "That is not your place, Claudia!" he yelled in Italian. His heavy eyebrows joined to form one dark line across his forehead. Rosa stepped back.

Uncle Sal put his hand on Papa's shoulder, but Papa brushed him away and said, "You seem to forget, Claudia—you are the youngest." Papa pointed at her. "And a woman! You have no right to tell Pa what to do."

Aunt Claudia's face flushed bright red. "I can say whatever I want to my own father!" she shot back in Italian. "And I'm not going to stay here and let you or anyone else tell me otherwise!" Aunt Claudia stood up. "Primo, Enzo, get our coats. We're going home."

"But, Mama," Primo started to protest.

Uncle Mario interrupted him. "Do what your mama says."

Ma and Aunt Ida came into the dining room

just as Primo and Enzo returned with the coats. "What's this?" Ma said.

"Claudia is leaving," Papa said.

Ma looked confused. "I thought we were all going to midnight Mass together."

"She wants to leave now," Papa said.

Ma turned to Aunt Claudia, who was standing with her back to Papa. Before either woman could speak, Uncle Mario said, "It's best we go." He helped Aunt Claudia into her coat.

While everyone else said hurried goodbyes, Aunt Claudia and Papa avoided each other.

After Aunt Claudia's family left, Ma scowled at Papa. She must have guessed that he'd caused some trouble. But all she said was, "We might as well leave for church now. That way we'll get good seats." For Ma, midnight Mass was as important a Christmas Eve tradition as their meatless dinner. Not even a family argument could keep them from church tonight.

They were soon sitting in a pew, waiting for the pre-Mass carols to begin. The only light in the church came from the altar candles and the glowing red EXIT signs above the doors. In the hushed dimness, Rosa thought about what had happened that evening. When she recalled how Papa had spoken to his sister, Rosa's face grew hot. Papa'd had no right to boss Aunt Claudia that way.

But Rosa felt angry with Aunt Claudia, too. Why did her aunt have to get so upset about Nonno changing his will? Rosa didn't care what her grandfather did with his property. She'd probably never see his house or olive grove. If Nonno wanted to leave his olive trees to the baby, that was fine by Rosa. All that mattered was that she wouldn't be an only child anymore.

Music interrupted Rosa's thoughts. The choir started the caroling with "Silent Night." When she heard the words "'round yon Virgin Mother and Child, Holy Infant so tender and mild,"

Rosa pictured the Blessed Mother cradling baby Jesus in her arms. Rosa closed her eyes and thought of how she'd felt the first time she'd held Antonio. She remembered the softness of his cheek, and the tingling feeling that had spread through her whole body when he'd wrapped his hand around her little finger. That feeling had led Rosa to ask God for a brother just like Antonio.

The song ended and Rosa opened her eyes. She still wanted that brother. Yet now she worried about what would happen if God answered her prayers. Papa and Aunt Claudia had had terrible arguments before, but they always made up eventually. Would they be able to make up this time if Nonno changed his will? Or would Papa and Aunt Claudia never speak to each other again? Rosa didn't want her prayers for a brother to cost Papa a sister.

The music started again, and the lights slowly came on. The choir began singing "It

Came Upon a Midnight Clear." As the words "peace on the earth" echoed through the church, Rosa stared up at the crucifix above the altar and asked God to bring peace to her family.

6 ❧

Baby Picture

ROSA'S FAMILY DIDN'T get home from church till almost one-thirty in the morning. Yet Rosa still woke early Christmas day. Her first thoughts weren't of presents, though, but of Papa's argument with Aunt Claudia.

Rosa tried to push the thoughts from her mind as she dragged herself to the living room. When she saw what Santa had left for her, she gasped and forgot all about the argument. There, under the Christmas tree, stood a shiny red bicycle. "I can't believe it," Rosa exclaimed. "My very own bike!"

Papa was sitting in the recliner, reading the newspaper. He looked around the side of the paper and pretended to be surprised. "Oh my!" he said. "You must have been a good girl this year."

Ma smiled and put a hand on Rosa's shoulder. "A very good girl."

Rosa sat on the bicycle seat. The only bike she'd ever ridden was AnnaMaria's, but hers still had training wheels. This was a real two-wheeler! "My very own bike," Rosa repeated, stroking the yellow, red, and blue streamers attached to the ends of the handles. "Can I take it for a ride?" She looked up at Ma. "Please!"

"I can't help you." Ma touched the bulge of her maternity dress. "You'll have to ask your father."

"Can I, Papa?"

"I don't know," Papa said, hiding behind his paper. *"Fa freddo."*

"It's not that cold out." Rosa got off the bike

and walked over to the recliner. "Please, Papa. Pleeeease!"

Papa laughed. He folded the newspaper. "Of course you can ride it." He stood up, and Rosa saw that he was all dressed and ready to go. He ruffled her hair. "What are you waiting for, Rosalina?"

Rosa had never dressed so quickly. As she put on her coat and hat, Papa carried the bike outside and set it on the front sidewalk. The little snow that had fallen the week before had melted, so the walks were all dry.

Rosa stood beside her bike. In her excitement, she'd forgotten that she'd never ridden without training wheels. "What do I do?"

"Get on," Papa said. "I'll help you."

Papa held the bike while Rosa got on. Then he put one hand on the handlebar and the other on the seat, just behind Rosa. "Start pedaling," he said. "I'll support you."

Rosa pedaled a moment, but the bike wobbled so much she felt sure she'd fall. She put her feet on the ground. "I'm scared."

"Let me show you something." Papa let go of the handlebar. "Hold up your hand." Rosa did as he said. Papa slipped off her mitten and placed his bare hand against hers. His hand was much longer and wider than Rosa's. And she could feel the hard calluses on his palm. He raised his other hand. "With these big, strong hands holding you, I promise — you will not fall."

"Okay," Rosa said. She tried again. This time, when the bike wobbled, she adjusted the handlebar to regain her balance.

"That's it," Papa said.

Papa kept his promise. Rosa didn't fall. Before long, Papa was running alongside her with only one hand on the back of her seat.

Rosa was getting better at keeping her balance, but she still felt shaky. "Don't let go, Papa."

"I won't let go," Papa said between breaths, "till you say so."

Rosa found it easier to balance when she pedaled faster, but Papa was having a harder time keeping up. When they reached the corner he said, "I need . . . to rest." His words came out in little puffs.

Rosa stopped. She noticed that, despite the cold, sweat was running down Papa's cheeks.

"You're doing great," Papa said, drying the sweat with his coat sleeve. "Are you ready to try without me?"

Rosa shook her head. "Not yet, Papa. Just a little longer."

Papa nodded. "All right." He took a deep breath. "Let's try again."

They turned the bike around and started over. Halfway down the block, Rosa didn't feel Papa holding her anymore.

"Are you still there, Papa?"

"I'm here," he said.

Rosa swallowed hard. "Then let go." She pedaled faster. A shiver of excitement ran through her. The bike kept going. Rosa wobbled a bit, but didn't fall.

Still running beside her, Papa waved both his hands. She really was riding on her own!

Rosa stopped when she reached the corner. She was sweating almost as much as Papa.

"You did it, Rosa!" Papa said, running up to her. "You rode all by yourself."

Rosa hopped off and propped the bike on the kickstand. "I did it!" she said. She hugged Papa. "I really did it!"

Papa laughed. He lifted Rosa off the ground and spun her in a circle till she felt dizzy.

When he set her down, Rosa leaned against Papa to steady herself. "Thank you, Papa," she said. "You're the best."

Rosa rode her bike as much as she could the next two days. Then snow came, followed by bitter cold. Stuck inside again, she went back to "baby watching." But with Ma wearing maternity clothes now, it was harder to see the changes in her. Rosa took to patting Ma's belly every chance she got.

Rosa wished she could make April 28 come sooner. On New Year's Eve, she made a calendar to count the days till the baby's due date. Still 117 days to go!

By March 27th, the first day of Easter break, Rosa had marked off eighty-five of those days. Ma's belly had grown so big, Rosa wondered how she'd manage another month.

After breakfast that morning, Ma said, "Rosa, it is time for you to learn to wash clothes. There will be lots of laundry after the baby comes."

"Okay," Rosa answered.

Their old-fashioned wringer washer was already rumbling away when they reached the basement laundry room. "I started a load of diapers," Ma said. "So they will be all ready for the baby. I'll show you how to wring them out."

Ma stopped the washer and lifted a diaper from the tub. "You put the edge of the cloth next to the wringer like this," Ma said. "But keep your fingers far from the rollers. Then push the button." Ma pressed the button, and the end of the diaper disappeared between the rotating rollers. When the diaper came out the other side, it looked like Bugs Bunny after he'd been run over by a steamroller.

Rosa giggled. "That looks funny." The flattened diaper fell into the rinse tub. "Can I do the next one?"

Ma smiled. "Sure. Go ahead."

They rinsed the diapers twice, running them through the wringer again before and after the last rinse. Then Rosa carried the basket of squashed-out diapers to the clothesline on the other side of the basement. Ma showed her how to whip out the wrinkles. It took Rosa several tries before she snapped the diaper hard enough to make the same loud *thwack* Ma had.

"Good job," Ma said, and handed her a clothespin. Then she clutched her side. "He sure is kicking today."

Ma had never called the baby "he" before. "Do you think it's a boy?" Rosa asked.

"Yes," Ma said.

"Why?"

"Because of how I'm carrying." Ma stroked the outline of her bulging belly. "All in front. With you, I was much wider."

Rosa turned to pin the diaper to the clothesline. Could that be why Ma looked so big, because she was carrying a boy? Rosa smiled. A brother would be the answer to her prayers. But then she remembered Christmas Eve. Papa and Aunt Claudia hadn't spoken to each other since then.

"What about Aunt Claudia? If it *is* a boy, will she ever make up with Papa?"

"Your aunt will be fine." Ma handed Rosa another clothespin. "Claudia fusses a lot, but she doesn't hold on to her anger the way your papa does. I'm sure she'll be the first to visit after the baby comes, no matter if it's a boy or a girl."

As Rosa clipped the second pin to the diaper, Ma went on. "Of course, Claudia will expect to be godmother. She was *furiosa* when we picked Uncle Sal and Aunt Ida for your *compare* and *comare.* But by the day of your baptism, all was forgiven. That's how she is."

Rosa didn't know Aunt Claudia had wanted to be her godmother. If Aunt Claudia could forgive not being given that honor, she could forgive just about anything. "Are you going to ask her to be the baby's godmother?"

"I don't know yet. First your papa and I have to agree on a name," Ma said. "He wants to call the baby Pasquale, after his father."

Rosa didn't particularly like the idea of naming her brother after Nonno. Her grandfather's letter had started all the trouble at Christmas. Besides, Rosa didn't even know how to say Nonno's name in English. "Is Pasquale the same as Peter?"

Ma shook her head. "Peter is Pietro."

Rosa took another diaper from the basket as Ma said, "Pasquale is Pasquale. There is no such name in English."

"You can't do that to the baby, Ma." Rosa whipped the diaper so hard it *thwacked* on the first try. "He'd be the only Pasquale in the whole school. All the kids would make fun of him."

"Don't worry so, Rosa." Ma put her arm around Rosa's shoulders, giving her a sideways hug. "Nothing is settled yet. I want to name the baby Joseph, like your papa."

"That would be much better," Rosa said. She knew at least three Josephs at Our Lady of Mercy School. "Everyone knows how to spell Joseph. *I* don't even know how to spell Pasquale."

Ma laughed. "And you are so good in spelling now."

Rosa laughed, too. Her spelling really had improved, thanks to Ma's help. Rosa had even taken third place in last year's classroom spelling bee. "Well, *I* could probably figure out how to spell Pasquale," she said. "But no one else would."

After they'd finished hanging the diapers, Ma said, "While we are down here, let's bring up the baby bed."

Ma found Rosa's old bassinet in the basement storeroom. Rosa helped her carry it upstairs and set it up in the corner of Ma's bedroom. "Whew, it is dusty," Ma said, brushing her hands together. "Run and get a dishrag and some water."

Rosa brought two dishrags. While Ma washed the hood of the white wicker basket, Rosa squatted down and did the legs. With the sun streaming in the bedroom window, Ma began singing "You Are My Sunshine," one of the few American songs she knew.

Rosa joined in on the second line, "You make me happy when skies are gray." As their voices rose, Rosa felt the happiness rise up inside her. "You'll never know dear, how much I love you," they sang together. "Please don't take my sunshine away."

When the bassinet was clean, Rosa looked down into it. The baby bed seemed so much smaller than Antonio's crib. "Will the baby fit in there?"

Ma laughed. "Of course. You did." Ma set her dishrag on top of the bassinet hood. "I'll show you." She went to her triple dresser and reached for the handle of the bottom drawer, but her belly got in the way.

"I'll get it, Ma." Rosa opened the drawer and pulled out the shoebox that held the family photographs.

"*Grazie,*" Ma said. She carried the box to the dining room, where she placed it on the table. Ma sat down and sifted through the pictures. Rosa stood beside her.

"Here it is." Ma handed Rosa an old black-and-white photograph. "That is you, in the bassinet."

Rosa looked at the tiny baby wrapped in a blanket. "That's me?"

Ma nodded. "You were only one week old."

Rosa could hardly believe she'd ever been that small. But she recognized Lamby, the stuffed lamb lying beside her in the bassinet. "I sure had a lot of hair," Rosa said.

Ma nodded. "You cannot tell from the

photo, but your eyes were *azzurri*. Blue as the water of Lake Michigan."

Rosa turned to Ma. "But my eyes are hazel, like yours."

"I know," Ma said. "They started out *azzurri*. Then, little by little, they got dark."

Rosa stared at the picture. When she had prayed for a brother, she'd always imagined him with big brown owl eyes, like Antonio's, and a bald head, too. How much more fun it would be if the baby looked like her. Then people could tell right away that he was her brother.

Rosa gave the picture back to Ma. "Do you think the baby will look like me? The way I did then?"

"We shall see," Ma said with a smile. "We shall see."

7 🌹

Birthday Presents

OVER A MONTH later, on the morning of her birthday, Rosa was still waiting to see what the baby looked like. She fidgeted impatiently as Ma squeezed red icing onto her birthday cake. Ma's belly was now so big she had to lean sideways to reach the counter. And in the heat of the kitchen, her cheeks had flushed as red as the number ten she was writing. "This *bambino* is lucky," Ma said as she worked, "to have such a grown-up sister."

"The baby's already a day late," Rosa said, the vinyl kitchen chair squeaking under her. "When will he be born?" She still felt odd calling the baby "he" without knowing for sure it was a boy. But that's what Ma'd been calling him for the last month.

"If he doesn't come soon," Ma said, "the doctor will make him come on Monday."

Rosa said a silent prayer that the baby would be born today, on her birthday. That would be the best present of all.

Ma pushed the cake to the back of the counter, then turned to the table. She lifted the blue linen towel covering a mound of rising dough. "Time to do the bread."

The smell of yeast mingled with the sweet aroma of birthday cake as Ma kneaded the bread dough. Suddenly, she shut her eyes and leaned into the table. The red flush drained from her cheeks.

Rosa jumped up. "Ma, are you okay?"

Ma took a deep breath, then exhaled

through her mouth. "It's nothing." She rubbed the apron that covered her bulging belly, leaving white streaks on the brown cloth. Opening her eyes, she fanned her face with her hand. "It's just warm in here." Ma pointed at the door to the back porch. "Let some air in, Rosa."

Swallowing the fear in her throat, Rosa opened the kitchen door. Then she walked out on the porch and unlocked the heavy porch door. A cool April breeze swept in through the screen.

Back in the kitchen, Rosa opened the windows, too. The yellow-and-white checked curtains fluttered in the breeze, but Ma still looked pale. Maybe she was working too hard. While the birthday cake had been baking, Ma had scrubbed the linoleum kitchen floor on her hands and knees.

Rosa stood by feeling helpless. She wished she knew how to make bread so she could take over for Ma.

Ma nodded toward the cupboard beside the stove. "Get the bread pans."

Rosa placed the pans on the table, next to the wooden bread-making board. Ma took another long breath. Then she scooped some flour from the canister to coat her hands. Flour dust floated onto the dough as Ma cut off a hunk and set it aside for their supper pizza. She punched down what was left of the mound and began kneading the dough, pressing so hard that the metal legs of the Formica table creaked. Drops of sweat formed at her temples, where her brown hair curled over her cheeks.

The color gradually returned to Ma's face as she worked. Relieved, Rosa grabbed the frosting bowl and sat down again. She scraped out the leftover icing with her fingers, then let the sweet frosting dissolve in her mouth.

In no time at all, Ma divided the dough into six loaves, kneaded the loaves, and placed them into the pans. "Rosa," she said, covering the pans with the blue towel, "go dust the living and dining room before your papa gets home."

"Yes, Ma." Rosa hurried off. She knew Ma

wanted everything in order before their company arrived after supper.

As Rosa dusted the backs of the dining-room chairs, she realized she would be the only kid at her birthday celebration. Her parents didn't follow the American custom of inviting friends — birthday parties were strictly for family. Normally, Rosa didn't mind, because her cousins were usually here. But Papa and Aunt Claudia still weren't speaking to each other. Only Uncle Sal and Aunt Ida were coming tonight.

Then Rosa remembered what Ma had said about Aunt Claudia, that she would be the first to visit after the baby arrived. Rosa smiled. That wouldn't be long now.

Rosa and Ma had just finished cleaning up supper when the front doorbell rang. Papa led his aunt and uncle into the dining room.

"Ah, here's the birthday girl," Uncle Sal said when he saw Rosa. He kissed her on both cheeks, as usual. "You're growing up too fast," he said, shaking his head.

Papa said, "I know," then smiled. "Soon we won't be able to call her Rosalina anymore."

"You can always call me Rosalina, Papa." She still liked his pet name for her, even though it meant *little* Rosa.

Aunt Ida waved Uncle Sal aside so she could give Rosa one of her pretend kisses. "Here you are, child." She handed Rosa a small box wrapped in stiff gold-colored paper. "Happy birthday."

Papa pulled out one of the dining-room chairs. "Please, sit," he said to Aunt Ida. "Wait till you see the cake Frannie made."

Ma headed for the kitchen. "*Vieni*, Rosa."

Rosa placed the present from Aunt Ida on the dining room table, then followed.

In the kitchen, Ma filled the *espresso* maker with water. "Get me the coffee, Rosa."

Rosa went to the pantry for the special *espresso* Ma saved for company. When Rosa came back into the kitchen, Ma was leaning against the counter. Her face was pale again, the way it had been after decorating Rosa's cake.

Rosa's stomach tightened. "Here, Ma." Rosa pulled a chair next to her mother. "Sit down."

This time Ma sat without arguing.

"Should I get Papa?"

Ma shook her head. "Our guests are waiting." She pointed at the demitasses on the counter. The white porcelain cups were half the size of regular coffee cups, made just for drinking *espresso.*

Rosa placed the cups and saucers on the silver serving tray Aunt Ida had given Ma and Papa when they bought the two-flat. Then Rosa added the sugar bowl, cake plates, and silverware. As she carried the tray to the dining room, Rosa glanced at Ma again. Ma waved for her to hurry.

By the time Rosa returned to the kitchen, Ma had started the coffee and was putting the candles on the cake.

"Are you okay now, Ma?"

"I am fine." Ma put a hand on Rosa's shoulder. "You worry too much. Go sit down."

Ma carried the cake into the dining room with all the candles lit and set it in front of Rosa. Everyone sang "Happy Birthday." Then Ma said, "Go ahead, Rosa. Make a wish."

Rosa stared into the quivering flames. She knew exactly what her wish would be. As she blew out the candles, Rosa thought, *I wish for the baby to be born today, on my birthday.* Then she'd finally know if it was the brother she'd prayed so hard for.

Rosa opened the present from her parents first. "Wow! A baseball mitt!" She breathed in the mitt's new-leather smell.

"Your old glove was getting small," Papa said. "How's this one fit?"

Rosa slid her left hand into the mitt. "It's perfect. Thank you." She kissed Papa, then Ma.

Rosa made a fist with her right hand and punched it into the mitt. "Can we try it out tonight, Papa?"

Papa laughed. "It's too dark. We'll try it tomorrow," he said. "But don't throw the old glove away. We can save it for the baby."

Rosa grinned. She could hardly wait till the baby was big enough to play catch with her.

"Aren't you going to open *my* gift, Rosa?" Aunt Ida asked.

Rosa nodded, slipping the mitt from her hand. She forced herself to smile as she unwrapped the gold-colored paper. Aunt Ida had a habit of giving Rosa gifts she hated. Last year, it had been an ugly olive-green vest, two sizes too large.

This time, Rosa opened the box to find a small baby doll, with its own tiny plastic bottle. Rosa held up the doll. It wasn't much bigger than her hand — the kind of doll a two-year-old might like.

Rosa kept the smile on her face as she said, "Thank you, Aunt Ida."

Aunt Ida smiled, too. "You can play with your doll baby when your mama takes care of her baby."

Rosa turned and shoved the doll back into the box. She wouldn't need a doll baby. She was going to help with the real one.

After Uncle Sal and Aunt Ida left, Rosa carried the cups and plates to the kitchen. She found Ma sitting at the table holding her belly, her face tight. "Is it time for the baby to come now, Ma?" Rosa asked, feeling hopeful and worried at the same time.

Ma shook her head. "The pains are not regular yet. Maybe later tonight." Ma took a deep breath, then stood. "If I have to go to the hospital while you're asleep, Mrs. Graziano will come over from next door. Now you get ready for bed."

After brushing her teeth, Rosa decided to sneak one more look at the baby bassinet. She tiptoed to the dining room. Her parents were watching the news in the living room, their backs to Rosa. She crept into their bedroom.

As she shut the bedroom door, Rosa's arm brushed the plastic bag holding Papa's navy blue suit. Papa must have left the suit hanging on the door after picking it up from the cleaner's. He owned only two suits: the blue one for weddings and baptisms, and a charcoal gray one for wakes and funerals. Rosa smiled. The blue one was all ready for the baby's baptism.

The wicker bassinet still stood in the far corner, on Ma's side of the bed. Peeking under the hood, Rosa saw that Ma had covered the miniature mattress with a white sheet. A green-and-white checked blanket lay folded neatly at the foot of the baby bed. Rosa stroked the fuzzy blanket and wondered if it had been hers, too. She still had a hard time believing she'd ever slept in such a small bed. She thought of the picture Ma had shown her. Would the baby have the same blue eyes Rosa'd had? Would he look as tiny lying in the bassinet with Lamby?

That's what was missing. Lamby. Rosa hurried to her room. Lamby sat in his usual spot, balanced on her headboard. Now that she was ten, she no longer needed her stuffed friend to watch over her. It was time to give Lamby to the baby.

Back in Ma's room, Rosa hugged Lamby, pressing her face into his soft fur. Then she laid him in the bassinet. Lamby's fur looked gray against the white sheet, and his yellow hooves were faded and worn. But he still had lots of love to give. Rosa covered Lamby with the checked blanket, then bent down and whispered, "Don't worry, Lamby. You won't be alone long."

8 ✿

May Day

ROSA'S BIRTHDAY WISH did not come true. When she got up the next morning, Ma was still in bed. Ma's labor pains had kept her awake much of the night, but they weren't regular enough for Ma to go to the hospital.

By breakfast, the pains had stopped altogether and Ma started to get ready for church. Papa stopped her, though. He insisted she stay home in case her labor started again.

Rosa watched Ma closely all day, but the pains never returned. Rosa didn't know if that was good or bad. She asked Ma about it Sunday evening, while they were doing dishes. "I don't know," Ma said with a shrug. "One way or another, the baby will be born soon. I see the doctor at ten tomorrow morning." Ma turned to Rosa and smiled. "Maybe it is *destino*. Your papa will have to let me name the baby Joseph if he is born tomorrow. It is a feast day for Saint Joseph."

"What if it's a girl?" Rosa asked.

"Then we'll call her Josephina."

Rosa smiled. Tomorrow she'd finally find out if God had sent the brother she'd prayed so hard for.

Monday morning, Rosa woke to the smell of something burning. She opened her bedroom door to find Mrs. Graziano in the kitchen. Rosa watched her tiny, gray-haired neighbor toss two pieces of toast into the trash. The bread was burned as black as Mrs. Graziano's widow's dress.

"Where's Ma?" Rosa asked.

Mrs. Graziano looked up. "Oh, *buon giorno*, Rosa." In spite of her smile, Mrs. Graziano's eyes looked worried. "Your mama, she is at *l'ospedale*, having her baby." Mrs. Graziano turned to put two more slices of bread in the toaster.

"Why'd she go so early?" Rosa asked. "Her appointment wasn't till ten."

Keeping her back to Rosa, Mrs. Graziano said, "She could not wait. Her labor started in the middle of the night."

Rosa got the feeling Mrs. Graziano was hiding something. "Is everything okay?"

"Of course." This time the toast popped up too soon, but Mrs. Graziano buttered it anyway. She set the plate on the table. "Sit and eat, Rosa, or you will be late for *scuola*."

As she bit into her toast, Rosa prayed everything really was okay.

Sister Mary Ambrose, Rosa's fourth-grade teacher, was the youngest nun Rosa had ever met. Sister Ambrose had the most beautiful smile, too — her teeth were as bright as the white cloth that framed her face. She had quickly become Rosa's favorite teacher.

This morning, Sister started class as usual, with the Pledge of Allegiance. Then she flipped the giant wall calendar to the next page. "Today is May Day," Sister said. "And the feast of Saint Joseph the Worker."

Rosa smiled, remembering what Ma had said. Papa would have to name the baby Joseph now. Or Josephina.

As Sister Ambrose told the class about Saint Joseph, Rosa decided to ask for the Saint's intercession. She closed her eyes and prayed in her mind, "Dear Saint Joseph, please watch over baby Joseph or Josephina today, on your feast day. And Ma, too."

"Rosa, are you all right?" she heard Sister say.

Rosa opened her eyes. "Yes, Sister."

"Good. Then take out your math book and turn to page 103."

Rosa finished the math problems quickly,

then glanced up at the clock. Only nine-thirty. Had the baby been born yet? Was it a boy? What did he look like?

The hours dragged on. Rosa tried not to watch the clock, but she couldn't help herself. At two-thirty, she thought, *Papa must surely be home by now.* He was probably sitting on the back porch, waiting to tell her the news. Or maybe he'd meet her out front and take Rosa to the hospital to see the baby right away.

Rosa was so wrapped up in her thoughts that when the bell finally did ring, it startled her. She jumped up, grabbed her things, and ran all the way home.

She made it home in record time, but there was no sign of Papa out front. Rosa hurried around back. He wasn't on the porch either. She burst through the kitchen door, then came to a sudden stop. There, sitting at Papa's place at the head of the table, was Aunt Ida.

"Where's Papa?" Rosa asked, fighting to catch her breath. She set her book bag on the table and looked around. "Where's Uncle Sal?"

Something was wrong. Aunt Ida never came over without Uncle Sal. "What's happened?"

Aunt Ida stood up. "Now, Rosa, I have some bad news." She put her arm around Rosa. "You're going to have to be strong."

Rosa didn't want to be strong. She brushed away Aunt Ida's arm.

"*Mi dispiace*, Rosa," Aunt Ida went on. "I wish I did not have to be the one to tell you, but Salvatore had to . . ." She seemed to be fumbling for words. "He had business to attend to." Aunt Ida sat back down. "And your papa needs to be with your mama right now."

Rosa's stomach went cold. She swallowed to keep the panic from creeping up into her throat. "What's wrong with Ma?"

Aunt Ida was quiet for what seemed an eternity. A voice in Rosa's head whispered, *Tell me Ma's fine. Tell me she'll be home soon. Tell me everything will be okay.*

Finally, Aunt Ida said, "Your mama had a very hard time, Rosa. There were complications with the delivery. She started bleeding and the doctors couldn't stop it. They had to perform emergency surgery."

Complications? Rosa didn't understand. Ma had said everything would be fine. She said Nonna had seven children without any trouble. *Why should Ma be any different?*

Rosa tried to swallow again, but the fear felt like a lump of ice in her throat. She wet her lips so she could talk. "Is Ma okay?"

Aunt Ida took Rosa's hand and pulled her to the chair. "So far, your mama's holding her own, but she lost a lot of blood. We have to wait and see how she recovers."

The panic melted back into Rosa's stomach. Ma's alive.

Aunt Ida put on a smile and patted Rosa's hand. "Your mama is tough. I feel sure she will come through this all right."

Rosa nodded. Ma *was* strong. She never got sick.

Then Aunt Ida's smile slipped away and she looked down at Rosa's hand. "Forgive me,

Rosa." Aunt Ida's voice cracked. "I must give you more bad news."

No. No more bad news. Rosa yanked her hand from her godmother's grasp.

Before Rosa could cover her ears, Aunt Ida said, "The baby is dead."

"No," Rosa said. She shook her head hard, but she could already feel the tears in her eyes. "It can't be."

"I am so very sorry." Aunt Ida tried to pull her close. "He was stillborn."

Rosa pushed her godmother away. "Stillborn? What does that mean?"

"*È nato morto.* He was born dead."

How can a baby be born and be dead at the same time? As the thought flashed through Rosa's mind, she realized Aunt Ida had called the baby "he."

"The baby was a boy?"

Aunt Ida nodded.

NO! the voice in Rosa's head shouted. But she couldn't speak. The flood of tears rising up inside her poured out. This time, when Aunt Ida reached for her, Rosa didn't fight. She let Aunt Ida lift her onto her lap.

Rosa's sobs shook her whole body. *Why did Aunt Ida have to be the one to tell me? Why couldn't Papa be here? Or Uncle Sal? Or Aunt Claudia? Maybe then it wouldn't hurt so bad.*

Aunt Ida hugged her tight. Rosa tried to stop trembling. But even with Aunt Ida's arms around her, Rosa felt colder than she'd ever felt before. She pressed her body against her godmother's. Still, Rosa couldn't get warm.

Ma was the only one who could make the cold go away.

9

Gray Suit

EXHAUSTED FROM CRYING, Rosa went to bed. She slept till the phone woke her several hours later. Maybe it was all a dream, she thought. Maybe Ma was calling to tell Rosa about her new baby brother.

Rosa opened her bedroom door.

"Hello, Claudia," Aunt Ida said into the phone. "No, there's no news. . . . I don't know. He won't leave Francesca's side. Salvatore is at the hospital keeping an eye on him. I will stay here tonight."

Rosa shut the door. "He" had to be Papa. It was no dream.

Fresh tears formed in Rosa's eyes. She climbed back into bed. She cried silently, so Aunt Ida wouldn't hear. Rosa didn't want her godmother trying to comfort her. Aunt Ida could never understand. She didn't know how Rosa had prayed and prayed for a baby brother. Only Ma knew.

Rosa stayed in bed the rest of Monday and all of Tuesday. She saw only Aunt Ida and Mrs. Graziano — they took turns bringing her meals. Rosa wasn't hungry, but she ate anyway, just so they would leave her alone.

Wednesday morning she woke to the sound of thunder. Rain pounded her window for what seemed like hours. When it finally eased up, someone knocked at the back door.

Rosa heard muffled voices from the porch. Then, back in the kitchen, Aunt Ida said, "Sit down, Teresa. I will make tea."

"Grazie," Mrs. Graziano said. A chair scraped across the floor.

"So much rain!" Aunt Ida said. "I hope it stops for the funeral tomorrow."

Funeral? Rosa sat up. She'd never been to a funeral. She had gone to Mr. Graziano's wake the year before, though. Rosa had knelt in front of his dark oak coffin with Ma and Papa. The kind old man had looked asleep. But Rosa knew from watching his chest that he wasn't breathing.

Mrs. Graziano's voice interrupted Rosa's thoughts. "The Mass will be at Our Lady of Mercy?"

"Yes, at ten o'clock," Aunt Ida answered. "Salvatore has made all the arrangements."

Rosa hoped the new priest, Father Davis, would say the funeral Mass, and not old Monsignor Kelly. Either way, Monsignor had probably already told Sister Ambrose about the funeral. Tomorrow morning Sister would have Rosa's class pray for her brother, just as they had prayed for Bridget Sullivan's grandfather on the day of his funeral.

The teakettle whistled, then Rosa heard cups clinking.

"What name did they give him?" Mrs. Graziano asked.

"Joseph," Aunt Ida said. "Just as Francesca had wanted."

"Joseph," Rosa repeated softly. Would baby Joseph's coffin be open in church, the way Mr. Graziano's had been at the wake? Rosa hoped so. Then she'd at least know what her brother had looked like.

Late Wednesday night, Papa finally came home. A wave of relief washed over Rosa when she heard him in the kitchen.

She sat up and swung her legs over the side of the bed. But something in Papa's voice stopped her. "You can sleep in your own bed tonight, Aunt Ida," he said flatly. "Uncle Sal is waiting for you in the car." Papa sounded strange, different somehow.

"All right, Giuseppe," Aunt Ida said. "I'll see you in the morning." The kitchen door squeaked, then Aunt Ida said, "You get some rest—you look exhausted." Maybe it was Papa's tiredness that made him sound so different. As he walked down the hall to his room, Rosa decided not to bother him. She could wait till morning to see him.

Rosa rose early Thursday to prepare for the funeral. After eating a bowl of cold cereal, she went to her room and put on the new blue Easter dress Ma had made. As Rosa brushed the snarls from her tangled hair, she heard Papa shaving in the bathroom. But by the time she'd finished, he had already returned to his room.

Rosa was sitting at the dining-room table, waiting for Papa, when someone knocked at the back door.

"*Permesso?*" Aunt Ida called as she opened the door. "Can I come in?" She didn't wait for an answer.

Aunt Ida was dressed entirely in black—

91

black dress, black hose, black shoes. Rosa looked down at her own light blue dress and hoped it was okay for a funeral. Then she sat up taller. The dress would be just fine next to Papa's navy blue suit.

"What are you all dressed up for?" Aunt Ida said.

"The funeral," Rosa answered.

"But you're not going."

Not go? How could she not go to her own brother's funeral?

Aunt Ida sat down beside Rosa. "That's why I'm here. To stay with you while your papa's gone."

Rosa stared straight ahead at Papa's bedroom door. Aunt Ida didn't know anything. When Papa saw how grown-up Rosa looked, he'd surely let her go.

But when Papa opened his door, he was wearing the charcoal gray suit. A lump rose to Rosa's throat. This should have been a happy day. A day to celebrate her brother's birth. A blue suit day.

Rosa swallowed and stood up. Papa was already in the kitchen. Had he even noticed her?

As Rosa hurried to the kitchen, her tears fell onto the floor. "I want to go, too," she tried to call out, but her throat was too thick.

Papa wouldn't have heard anyway. He'd already gone out the door.

Aunt Ida grabbed Rosa from behind. "I told you, you cannot go, Rosalina."

"Don't call me that," Rosa said. "I'm not a baby anymore. Let go."

"No," Aunt Ida said. "A funeral is no place for a child."

Who did Aunt Ida think she was, telling her what to do? "I don't care." Rosa tried to pull away. She was strong for her age. If she fought hard enough, Rosa might still be able to catch Papa. "I want to go!" She stomped her foot. "I want to see my brother."

"You won't be able to see the baby," Aunt Ida said. "The *cofanetto* is closed."

Rosa stopped struggling. *I won't see him?* She took a breath. It didn't matter — she could see his coffin. And say goodbye. Rosa had never even said hello to her baby brother. At least she could say goodbye.

"I want to go to Mass," Rosa said, finally breaking free from Aunt Ida. "To pray for baby Joseph."

She had just reached the door when Aunt Ida said, "We can pray for him here. And for your mama, too."

Rosa turned around. "Why do we need to pray for Ma? You said she was going to be okay."

Aunt Ida hesitated, then said in a squeaky voice, "Sure, she is." She cleared her throat. "We should pray for her to recover quickly, that is all. So she can come home sooner."

Aunt Ida glanced around the room. Then she grabbed the statue sitting on top of the refrigerator—a white ceramic figure of the Blessed Mother holding the baby Jesus. Aunt Ida placed the statue in the middle of the kitchen table.

"We will pray to *la Madonna*," Aunt Ida said. She took Rosa's hand. "Come, kneel with me."

Rosa didn't want to kneel. She wanted to know about Ma. But Rosa knew Aunt Ida would never answer her questions, so she did as she was told.

Kneeling on the hard linoleum beside Aunt Ida, Rosa turned to face the statue of the Madonna and Child. *"Cara Madonna,"* Aunt Ida began, looking up toward the ceiling, "you know how much this child needs her mother." Aunt Ida put her hand on Rosa's shoulder. "Please intercede for Francesca, that she may get well and come home to her daughter soon."

Rosa put her hands together and pointed her fingers toward heaven, the way the sisters had taught her in school.

Aunt Ida prayed, "Hail Mary, full of grace, the Lord is with thee. . . ."

Rosa said the words along with her godmother — the same words Rosa had repeated over and over when she'd prayed for a baby brother. God had answered her prayers. Only now her brother was dead. Rosa's face flushed with anger. How could God let this happen?

Rosa tried to concentrate on the statue, but the bald baby Jesus reminded her of Antonio. Had Joseph looked like that, or had he looked like her? Rosa would never know now. She would never cuddle her baby brother in her arms. She would never feel his hand around her little finger.

As tears trickled down her cheeks, Rosa closed her eyes. She closed her mouth, too. She couldn't pray anymore.

10

Lost Lamb

AUNT IDA SAID at least ten Hail Marys. By the last one, Rosa felt numb. She got up from her knees and went to her room. After locking the door, she stood with her hand pressed against the dark oak door panel. If only she could have touched baby Joseph's coffin.

This was all Aunt Ida's fault! If not for her, Rosa could have gone to the funeral and said goodbye to her brother. Rosa's eyes filled with tears. She dropped onto her bed and sobbed. It didn't matter anymore if her godmother heard. Aunt Ida didn't really care about her.

Someone knocked on her door. "Rosa, are you okay?" Aunt Ida asked.

"I'm fine," Rosa answered, her voice husky. She reached for a tissue and blew her nose.

The doorknob jiggled. "Do you want something to eat?" Aunt Ida said. "I'll make whatever you like."

"I'm not hungry!" Rosa shouted. "Leave me alone."

Aunt Ida did just that.

Rosa lay staring at the ceiling when the doorbell rang. She heard Aunt Ida walk toward the front of the house. Curious, Rosa unlocked her door and peered down the hall. She was surprised to see Aunt Claudia at the front door. Then Rosa remembered what Ma had said about Aunt Claudia being the first to visit after the baby came. Ma was right, only now there was no baby.

Aunt Claudia came in carrying a large basket of fruit. She walked to the dining room and set it on the table, then turned to greet Aunt Ida. Even dressed in black, Aunt Claudia looked as big as ever. As she and Aunt Ida exchanged kisses, the doorbell rang again. Rosa crept closer to the dining room. She expected to see Uncle Mario, Primo, or Enzo. Instead, it was one of Ma's cousins, with his wife and two other people Rosa didn't recognize.

Rosa leaned against the wall, hoping the afternoon shadows would hide her. Visitors arrived one after another, each one bringing a gift of food or drink.

AnnaMaria's mother showed up with a large white cake box. As Aunt Ida made room for the box on the dining-room table, Rosa studied the assortment of food. Her stomach gurgled, reminding her that she hadn't eaten since breakfast.

"Such a tragedy," Mrs. Morelli said, placing her box on the table, "to lose not only this baby, but the possibility of ever having another."

Rosa froze. *Was Mrs. Morelli talking about*

Ma? Rosa held her breath, straining to hear every word.

Mrs. Morelli went on. "Rosa must be heartbroken."

"Perhaps it is a blessing," Aunt Ida said. "Francesca was getting old to be having babies."

They *were* talking about Ma. Rosa's throat tightened. She couldn't listen anymore. She ran back to her room and threw herself onto the bed.

"A blessing! How can she call it a blessing?" Rosa's angry tears fell onto her pillowcase. "Aunt Ida knew I'd never have another brother or sister, and she still didn't let me go to the funeral." Rosa pounded her pillow. "I hate her! I hate her! I hate her!"

Rosa got up and paced. She felt trapped, like a caged animal with nowhere to go. She thought of Aunt Claudia in the other room. Why couldn't Rosa's parents have picked Aunt Claudia to be her godmother? She would surely have let Rosa go to the funeral.

When Rosa tired of pacing, she sat down in her rocker and rocked and rocked till her legs ached. Finally, her anger spent, Rosa sat staring at her bed till someone knocked.

"Rosa, it's Aunt Claudia. Can I come in?"

Rosa stood and smoothed out her dress — the same dress she'd put on that morning to wear to the funeral. She unlocked the door.

"Rosa," Aunt Claudia said, wrapping her arms around her.

Rosa rested her face on her aunt's huge bosom. Aunt Claudia still smelled like lily of the valley. The familiar scent comforted Rosa.

When Rosa pulled away, Aunt Claudia said, "My, you are turning into a lovely young lady." She put her hand on Rosa's cheek. "I'm sorry I missed your birthday. You know, if it wasn't for that stubborn father of yours, I would have been here."

Rosa nodded. She wondered if Aunt Claudia had made up with Papa. With Joseph dead, they had nothing to argue about now.

Aunt Claudia said, "I bet you're hungry. How would you like a grilled mozzarella sandwich?"

"I'd like that a lot."

In the kitchen, Rosa noticed how quiet the house was. Everyone must have gone home. Rosa hoped Aunt Ida had left with them.

Aunt Claudia made not only one, but two sandwiches. "Careful," she said, as she set the plate of sandwiches on the kitchen table. "They're hot."

Rosa didn't realize how hungry she was until she took the first bite. The melted cheese tasted so good between the slices of crispy Italian bread. If the sandwiches hadn't been so hot, she would have gobbled them both down in a minute.

Aunt Claudia was bringing the fruit basket from the dining room when Papa walked in the back door. At the sight of his sister, Papa's forehead wrinkled into an angry scowl. "What are you doing here?"

Aunt Claudia placed the basket on the table. "I stayed to help Aunt Ida."

Uncle Sal came in behind Papa. Before Papa could say anything else, Uncle Sal said, "How good of you to help, Claudia. I am sure Ida appreciated it." He looked around the room. When he saw Rosa sitting at the table, he smiled and said, "Hello, Rosa."

Rosa smiled back. "Hi, Uncle Sal."

Uncle Sal asked Aunt Claudia, "Where is Ida?"

"She's lying down. Today's been very hard on her."

Ha, Rosa thought. *Aunt Ida's just faking it. She doesn't have any feelings.* If she did, she would have told Rosa the *whole* truth about Ma.

Aunt Claudia said to Papa, "You should have been here, Joe. You had a houseful."

"Oh, yeah? Well, I didn't ask them to come." Papa sat down across from Rosa. He still had on his gray suit, but it was rumpled now. His tie hung loose around his neck, and his shirt was unbuttoned at the top. His face looked different, darker somehow, as if covered by a shadow. He didn't seem to notice Rosa.

"They just wanted to pay their respects," Aunt Claudia said. "To give you their *condoglianze.*"

"I don't need anyone's sympathy," Papa said in an angry voice. "Least of all yours, Claudia." He glared at his sister. "I bet you're happy now — Pa won't be changing his will after all."

Aunt Claudia stepped back as if she'd been slapped. "How can you say such a thing?"

Rosa shrank into her chair. Why was her father being so mean?

Aunt Claudia opened her mouth to say something, but Uncle Sal spoke first. "It is the grief that makes you talk this way, Giuseppe," Uncle Sal said. "You know in your heart that we all share your sadness."

"You cannot share my sadness," Papa said, his voice quiet now. He looked down and rubbed the calluses on his hands. "You do not know what it is to lose your only son."

Rosa couldn't bear to see Papa like this. She ran over and hugged him. "You still have me, Papa."

"Rosa," Papa said, a bit startled. "Yes," he whispered in a raspy voice. "I still have you." He squeezed her tight.

No one spoke for several minutes. Finally, Aunt Claudia said, "I should be going." She placed a hand on Papa's shoulder. "Let me know if you need anything."

Papa nodded, but the shadow didn't leave his face. He released Rosa.

She got up and kissed Aunt Claudia goodbye.

"Goodbye, dear." Aunt Claudia touched Rosa's cheek again. "It was good to see you."

Uncle Sal said, "Let me walk you to the door, Claudia."

Rosa glanced at Papa. He'd gone back to staring at his hands. She followed her godfather to the living room.

At the front door, Aunt Claudia asked Uncle Sal, "How's Frannie?"

"The worst is over." He kissed Aunt Claudia goodbye. "They moved her out of intensive care this afternoon."

Aunt Claudia smiled. "That's good news."

Uncle Sal nodded. "Yes, it is."

Rosa didn't know what "intensive care" meant, but it sounded bad. She was relieved that Ma wasn't there anymore.

"*Ciao*," Aunt Claudia said.

"*Ciao*," Uncle Sal replied, then shut the door.

Before going back to the kitchen, Rosa asked, "Is Ma still in the hospital?"

"*Si*, Rosa," Uncle Sal said. "Just on a different floor."

"Does that mean I can go see her now?"

He shook his head. "I am sorry. You have to be twelve years old to visit someone in the hospital."

"Couldn't we just say I'm twelve?" Rosa said. "I'm pretty tall for my age."

Uncle Sal chuckled. "You are too smart for your own good." He patted Rosa's back. "It is better you wait till your mama comes home. She needs her rest now."

Aunt Ida must have heard them talking, because she came out of Papa's bedroom. She and Uncle Sal left soon afterward.

Back in the kitchen, Papa asked Rosa, "Did they feed you?"

Rosa nodded.

"Good." He took off his coat and tie. "I guess I should change." He started toward his room.

Rosa decided to change her clothes too. She shut her bedroom door and was about to slip off her dress when a loud bang came from Papa's room. Rosa opened her door to see Papa carrying the bassinet into the kitchen, an angry scowl on his face again.

Bang. The metal bassinet legs hit the kitchen door as he stepped out onto the back porch. Where was Papa taking the baby bed?

Rosa waited till he'd gone down the back stairs. Then she hurried out to the porch. Peeking over the porch windowsill, she watched

Papa carry the bassinet toward the alley. When he reached the garbage bin beside the garage, he lifted the baby bed above his head and hurled it. *Crash.* Rosa jumped. The bassinet legs made a horrible noise as they hit the steel trash cans.

How could Papa throw out the bassinet? The bed *she* had slept in? Rosa thought of Lamby. She'd left him in the bassinet for the baby. Had Papa thrown Lamby out with the bed?

Papa brushed his hands together and turned toward the house. Rosa hurried back to her room, but she left her door cracked open. Papa slammed the back door, then stomped over to the cupboard where he kept the wine. He took out the two-liter bottle, grabbed a glass, and went down the hall.

Rosa had to look for Lamby right away, before it got dark. When Papa reached the living room, she tiptoed out the back door. She ran to the alley, where she found the bassinet behind the trash bin. The empty wicker basket lay on an angle, with the green-and-white checked blanket hanging out. Streaks of garbage stained the sides of the bassinet, and the metal legs were bent. Rosa pulled out the blanket, but Lamby wasn't in it. She lifted the baby bed and looked underneath. No sign of Lamby anywhere.

Rosa set the bed back down. Buzzing flies swarmed over the exposed trash. The sight of them combined with the smell of rotting garbage made her stomach sick. Holding her nose with one hand, Rosa lifted the trash can lid from the ground and covered the garbage.

That's when she found Lamby, lying where the lid had been. Relieved, she picked him up. Except for a smudge between his eyes, he looked fine. "It's okay, Lamby," Rosa said, brushing his fur. "It's just a little dirt."

She looked back down at the bassinet. In the gathering dusk, the hood cast a shadow over the basket, making it look like a deep hole. Staring into the darkness felt like peering into a cave. A black, empty cave. Suddenly, Rosa felt as empty as the bassinet. She closed her eyes, but the memory of holding AnnaMaria's baby brother filled her mind. She saw again Antonio's owl eyes and bald head. And again Rosa wondered what her own brother had looked like. She opened her eyes and clutched Lamby tight, but the empty feeling wouldn't go away.

Back inside, Papa lay snoring on the living-room sofa, the wine half gone from the bottle. Rosa wondered if Papa felt the empty cave, too.

11 🌹

Bird Kisses

ROSA DIDN'T WAKE till after eight the next morning. The sky outside the kitchen windows looked gray, and the house felt cold. She knew she should eat something, but just the sight of the fruit basket on the table made her sick. The *tick-tick-tick* of the wall clock echoed inside her as she stood alone in the kitchen. She shivered, remembering the horrible empty-cave feeling of the day before. Rosa headed down the hall. Maybe watching TV would make the feeling go away.

In the living room, she found Papa's empty wine bottle lying on the floor. She'd heard him go to bed in the middle of the night. His bedroom door was still closed. Rosa picked up the bottle. Had drinking all that wine made Papa drunk? He usually had wine with dinner, but never that much. And he only stayed in bed this late on Sundays, or when he didn't feel good. Maybe Papa was sick. Rosa thought of Ma, all alone in the hospital, waiting for him. Rosa stared up at the ceiling and blinked back her tears. She'd done enough crying.

Rosa thought about knocking on Papa's door, to be sure he was okay. Then she remembered the look on his face when he'd carried the bassinet outside. She didn't want to risk making him angry again.

Rosa stood staring out the living-room window, trying to decide what to do, when Uncle Sal's car pulled up in front of the house. Rosa sighed with relief. She hurried to the kitchen and put the empty bottle in the sink.

When Rosa opened the back door to let Uncle Sal in, she saw that Aunt Ida was with him. Aunt Ida tried to give Rosa one of her pretend kisses, but Rosa moved away.

"Rosalina." Uncle Sal put a hand on her shoulder. "Are you okay?"

Rosa nodded, fighting tears once more. She didn't want Uncle Sal to think her a crybaby. "I'm okay. I'm just worried about Papa. He's still in bed."

"In bed? At this hour?" Uncle Sal said. "I thought we were going to the hospital together. Is he sick?"

"I don't know," Rosa said. "He drank a lot of wine last night."

"Wine?" Uncle Sal shook his head. "This is not good." He marched to Papa's room. Rosa followed.

Uncle Sal knocked on Papa's door. "Giuseppe, are you okay?"

"Go away," Papa said in an angry voice. "Leave me alone."

Ignoring Papa's words, Uncle Sal opened the bedroom door. "I want to talk to you," he said.

"Well, I don't want to talk to you, or anyone else."

Rosa cringed. If Papa yelled at her that way, she'd run and hide in her closet. It didn't seem to bother Uncle Sal, though. He walked into the room and closed the door behind him.

"Rosa," Aunt Ida called from the kitchen. "Where does your mama keep the *espresso*?"

Rosa wanted to stay and listen to what Uncle Sal said to Papa, but Aunt Ida called again, "Rosa!" Rosa trudged to the kitchen.

"Your papa needs a good strong cup of *espresso*," Aunt Ida said. "But this is all I can find." She held out a red can of Hills Brothers coffee.

Rosa went to the pantry and brought out the bag of imported coffee beans.

"Oh, very good." Aunt Ida took the bag from Rosa. "And the grinder?"

As Rosa opened the cupboard above the stove, she got the feeling Aunt Ida was keeping her in the kitchen so she wouldn't hear what Uncle Sal said to Papa. Rosa placed the coffee grinder on the counter. Before Aunt Ida could ask for it, Rosa took out the Italian coffeepot, too. "There," she said. "Anything else?"

"*Grazie*, Rosa."

Rosa had just started down the hall when Uncle Sal came out of Papa's room. Darn. Aunt Ida's plan had worked.

When Uncle Sal reached the kitchen, Aunt Ida asked, "So what did he say, Salvatore?"

Uncle Sal answered in Italian. "He is a very sad man."

"Sad?" Aunt Ida spoke in Italian, too. "He sounded *angry* to me."

Rosa reached for Ma's demitasses, pretending not to listen. As she placed the cups on the table, Uncle Sal sat down and said, "The anger keeps him from feeling the heartache."

Heartache. Rosa thought about the word.

Was that the empty-cave feeling? Then Papa did have it too.

"I asked him to let us take the child home," Uncle Sal said to Aunt Ida. "But he refused. He said he can take care of her himself."

"Ha," said Aunt Ida. She held up the empty wine bottle Rosa had left in the sink. "He hasn't been doing a very good job."

Rosa had never wanted to stay at Uncle Sal's and Aunt Ida's house before, but now, despite her anger at Aunt Ida, Rosa wished Papa had said yes. Maybe her heart wouldn't ache so much there.

Uncle Sal grabbed a red apple from the fruit basket and said in English, "Rosa, are red delicious still your favorite?"

Rosa shrugged. The tightness in her stomach made it hard to think about eating.

"Let us see if it is any good."

Uncle Sal took out his pearl-handled pocket knife and opened the blade with a loud snap. He cut the apple into fourths, then split one fourth in half the long way. He pared it carefully, removing the peel in one strip. Uncle Sal handed the apple section to her. "Try it," he said.

The apple crunched as Rosa bit into it, squirting sweet juice onto her tongue.

"How is it?" Uncle Sal asked.

Rosa swallowed. "Very good."

Uncle Sal smiled. "Good."

Outside, the sky had cleared, so sunlight now streamed in the windows. The light bounced off Uncle Sal's knife and danced on the ceiling as he cut and pared the rest of the apple. As soon as he finished a section, Rosa ate it. Meanwhile, the Italian coffeepot gurgled and hissed. The smell of *espresso* filled the air.

Aunt Ida set a glass of milk in front of Rosa.

"Ah, *latte*," Uncle Sal said. "Rosa, did you know birds like milk?"

"Huh?"

"*Sì*, it is true." Uncle Sal nodded. His face was serious, but his eyes twinkled. "I will show you." He picked up a piece of apple peel and folded the pointed end back about an inch.

Holding the peel over the edge of the glass, he squeezed the lower portion so that the top jerked back and forth. The pointed tip looked like a bird's beak as it bobbed toward the milk.

"Mmmmm. Tweet, tweet," Uncle Sal said in a squeaky voice. The apple peel puppet dipped up and down. "This milk is good. You should try some, little girl."

Uncle Sal sounded so silly, and the puppet looked so funny, Rosa couldn't help smiling.

Aunt Ida smiled, too. "You better drink that milk, Rosa," she said, "before the bird does."

Rosa swallowed the last of her apple, then took a large gulp of milk. It felt smooth and cold going down.

Uncle Sal made a second apple-peel puppet. Now two birds bobbed over the glass, one in each of his hands.

"Tweet, tweet. Who said you could have some milk?" the first bird said.

"It's a free country, isn't it? Chirp, chirp."

"But it belongs to the little girl," the first bird said. "You have to ask her."

Uncle Sal held the second bird in front of Rosa. "Chirp, chirp," he said in his funny bird voice. "May I please have some of your milk?" Uncle Sal turned the apple-peel puppet to one side so it looked like a bird cocking its head.

Rosa was giggling too hard to answer. She nodded instead.

"Oh, thank you." The bird kissed her cheek. Then the other bird joined in and Uncle Sal covered her face with bird kisses.

The kisses tickled. Rosa scrunched her head into her shoulders, laughing. She laughed till tears rolled down her cheeks. Soon, the trickle of tears turned into a steady flow. Rosa's eyes swelled, and her nose got so stuffy she could hardly breathe.

"It's okay, Rosalina," Uncle Sal said, rubbing her back. "Have yourself a good cry."

Rosa crossed her arms on the table and laid down her head. All the feelings she'd been holding inside came pouring out. For a while, she feared the tears would never end. But Uncle Sal kept rubbing her back and murmuring, "It's okay, Rosalina. It's okay." Gradually, the tears slowed, then finally stopped.

Uncle Sal pulled a large white handkerchief from his back pocket and gave it to Rosa. She blew her nose long and hard, then dried her face and arms.

Taking a deep breath, she turned to Uncle Sal. "Thank you," she said, her voice thick. She offered the handkerchief to her godfather.

Uncle Sal held up his hand. "You keep it." He smiled and added, "Next time you use it, think of me." Uncle Sal laughed.

Rosa smiled. Her eyes burned and her nose was clogged, but inside, she felt better, somehow lighter.

12 🥀

Old Spice

"THE COFFEE SMELLS good," Papa said.

Rosa looked up to see her father standing next to the fridge. She wondered how long he'd been there. Had he seen her crying? She quickly slid her hands under the table to hide Uncle Sal's handkerchief.

"I made it strong," Aunt Ida said. "The way you like it, Giuseppe."

Papa took his usual spot at the head of the table. He'd never changed out of yesterday's clothes. Now the collar of his white dress shirt stood up against his neck, making his morning stubble seem darker than usual. The shadow still lingered over his face, so Rosa couldn't tell whether he was angry, or sad.

Aunt Ida poured coffee into Papa's cup. He rubbed his hand over his face, as if brushing away cobwebs. "What day is it?"

"Friday, of course," Aunt Ida said.

Papa turned to Rosa. "Don't you have school?"

Rosa shrugged. She didn't want to think about school.

"That reminds me," Aunt Ida said. "The Morelli girl came by yesterday when you were resting, Rosa. She left some things for you. Let me find where I put them." Aunt Ida set the coffeepot on the stove and walked down the hall.

"Good," Papa said, scooping sugar into his *espresso*. "You can catch up on your homework before you go back to school Monday." He took a sip from the demitasse.

Go back to school? And face all the other kids? Rosa blurted out, "I don't want to go."

Papa looked at her over the top of his cup. "What do you mean, you don't want to go?"

Uncle Sal spoke more gently. "It will do you good, Rosa, to be around other children again."

That was the problem—Rosa didn't want to be around the other kids. She could already hear them whispering behind her back, "There goes poor Rosa. Did you hear about her brother?"

Aunt Ida placed Rosa's school things on the table. Seeing the pile of books and papers, Rosa said, "Can't I just do my schoolwork at home? The year's almost over."

"And who will take care of you when I go to work on Monday?" Papa said. He picked up his cup and swallowed the last of his coffee in one gulp. "I've already missed a week, and I will have to take time off again when your mama comes home."

Her hands still under the table, Rosa

squeezed Uncle Sal's handkerchief. She hoped Ma would be home soon so Papa could go back to being his old self.

Sunday morning, Rosa was lying awake in bed when the Collettis from upstairs trampled off to nine o'clock Mass, the way they did every Sunday. But this Sunday was different. This Sunday, Ma wasn't here to take Rosa to church.

Rosa knew Papa wouldn't take her — he went to church only on special days. Besides, Rosa wasn't sure she wanted to go. What could she say to God now, after everything that had happened? Part of her wanted to pray for Ma to get well, for Papa to be himself again, and for the empty-cave feeling to go away. But part of her never wanted to speak to God again. God had given her a brother only to take him away. How could she pray to a God like that?

Rolling over onto her side, Rosa felt the cross on her necklace slide toward the bed.

The gold cross and chain had been a baptism gift from Nonna Rosa and Nonno Pasquale. Rosa wore the necklace all the time, even in the bathtub. But today the cross seemed heavier than usual. Rosa sat up, unclasped the necklace, and set it on her nightstand. Then she went back to sleep.

On Monday, Papa left for work at his regular time, so he was gone long before Rosa got up. He had arranged for Mrs. Graziano to help Rosa get ready for school. As Rosa pulled on her jumper, Mrs. Graziano called from the kitchen, "Hurry, Rosa. You do not want to be late."

Mrs. Graziano was wrong—she did want to be late, to avoid meeting AnnaMaria on the way to school. Rosa feared she'd start crying again if her friend said anything about the baby. She didn't want to break down in front of any of the kids, not even AnnaMaria.

When Rosa reached their usual meeting spot, she looked up and down the street. No sign of AnnaMaria. Good.

As Rosa neared school, she heard kids shouting and laughing. She stopped in front of the church rectory and peeked around the corner. AnnaMaria stood with a group of girls near the school entrance. Not far from them, Mrs. Morelli and Mrs. Sullivan were talking, their two baby strollers parked between them.

AnnaMaria's mother was so busy talking, she didn't notice Antonio climbing out of his stroller. But Mrs. Sullivan saw him. He'd waddled only two steps away before she scooped him up and handed him to his mother. Rosa smiled. An older baby would have been able to make a clean getaway, but walking was new to Antonio — it was the first time she'd seen him walk on his own.

Then Rosa realized she would never see her own brother walk. The horrible emptiness came over her so suddenly she felt unsteady. She leaned against the cold red brick of the rectory and shut her eyes. Despite the bright sunshine, she shivered.

Rosa thought about going home, but she knew Papa wouldn't approve. There was no one home anyway.

Rosa took a deep breath and smelled something wonderful. She opened her eyes. On the corner stood a lilac bush, its purple blossoms dancing in the breeze. She walked to the bush. Rosa breathed in deeply until her body was filled with the sweet scent. By the time the bell rang, she felt calm enough to go inside.

Rosa made it through the morning by pretending she had blinders on, just like the horses in old photographs. She only let herself look up at Sister Ambrose or down at her desk. Rosa didn't want to see the other kids staring at her. She was different again — the only one in the class with a dead brother.

When it came time for spelling, Sister Ambrose said, "I have your tests here, class, and I'm pleased at how well you did." Sister smiled. Her sparkling white teeth made her whole face glow. Rosa couldn't help smiling back.

Sister's long, flowing habit swished as she walked down the aisles passing out tests. "Excellent job," Sister said, handing Rosa her test.

Rosa took the paper. Then Sister put a hand on Rosa's right shoulder and squeezed. The gesture surprised Rosa. She'd had perfect papers before without Sister squeezing her shoulder. Rosa glanced up. Sister's smile was gone, and her eyes looked sad.

Rosa turned away, afraid she might cry if Sister mentioned Joseph. Rosa's imaginary blinders fell off then, and she found herself facing AnnaMaria. AnnaMaria's eyes looked even sadder than Sister's. Before Rosa could look away, AnnaMaria mouthed the words, *I'm sorry.*

Rosa knew her friend was trying to be nice, but all she could think of was how AnnaMaria's brother was alive while hers was dead. The tears sprang up so fast, Rosa couldn't stop them.

"There, there," Sister said, patting her back. "It's all right." The teacher's tenderness made Rosa cry even harder.

Sister led Rosa into the hall. "I'm so sorry about your brother, Rosa." Sister reached into the pocket of her habit for a tissue. "It must be very hard for you to be here."

Rosa nodded. She felt so stupid for crying. The whole class was probably talking about her now. Rosa blew her nose into the tissue.

"Would you like me to call your father and ask him to take you home?"

Rosa shook her head. Between sniffles, she said, "He's at work."

"I see," Sister said. "Is there someone else I should call?"

Mrs. Graziano didn't drive. That left only Uncle Sal.

Rosa stuffed the soggy tissue into her jumper pocket and found Uncle Sal's handkerchief. She looked at the blue initials embroidered on the white cloth: SB. Salvatore

Bernardi. The handkerchief smelled of his Old Spice after-shave.

As Rosa blew her nose, she remembered Uncle Sal's words: *Next time you use it, think of me.* Rosa smiled. She dried her eyes with the handkerchief, folded it neatly, and tucked it back into her pocket. She said to Sister, "I'll be okay now."

13 ❧

Puzzle Pieces

SISTER AMBROSE LET Rosa eat lunch in the classroom, and Rosa stayed in for recess, too. That way the other kids couldn't make fun of her for crying. At least not to her face.

After school, Rosa hid in the girls' washroom to avoid AnnaMaria. When Rosa finally started for home, she remembered she couldn't go home. She had to go to Mrs. Graziano's.

Mrs. Graziano greeted her with milk and homemade *biscotti*. As Rosa bit into one of the almond cookies, Mrs. Graziano said, "Your papa called. He is going to *l'ospedale* after work, to sit with your mama awhile. So you can have supper with me." Mrs. Graziano smiled. "It will be nice to have company."

Rosa did her homework while Mrs. Graziano made supper. After they'd eaten and cleaned up, Mrs. Graziano said, "Would you like to help me with my puzzle? It is a tough one."

"Okay," Rosa said.

They went out to the back porch, where a jigsaw puzzle lay on an old wooden table. Mrs. Graziano showed Rosa the picture on the box. "The *Piazza San Marco* in *Venezia*," she said. "It is where Alberto and I had our honeymoon."

Rosa sat down. Mrs. Graziano had connected all the edge pieces, but not much else. Rosa picked up a sky-colored piece from a pile of blue ones sorted to one side. Mrs. Graziano started in on the gray building pieces. As they worked, Mrs. Graziano's yellow canary, Gelsomino, serenaded them. The bird's cheerful song lifted Rosa's spirits. She soon lost herself in the puzzle.

When Rosa heard a car door slam, she looked up to find that it was already dark outside. "That is your papa," Mrs. Graziano said as Papa stepped out the side door of his garage. "Let me give you some supper for him."

Rosa balanced Papa's supper on her book bag. "Thanks, Mrs. Graziano," she said, and hurried out.

At home, Rosa heated Papa's meal while he washed up. When he came into the kitchen, Rosa asked, "How's Ma?"

He shrugged without looking at her, then took his wine bottle from the cupboard.

Rosa waited, hoping he'd say something, but he sat down without speaking. She went to her room and got ready for bed.

Tuesday and Wednesday were just like Monday. Rosa continued to avoid AnnaMaria. When AnnaMaria tried to get her attention in class, Rosa pretended not to notice. She hoped she wasn't hurting AnnaMaria's feelings. Rosa told herself AnnaMaria was better off without her anyway. No one wants to be friends with someone who's different.

And Papa continued to avoid Rosa. She was used to not seeing him before school — he'd always left early for work. But now that he visited Ma every day, he didn't get home till long after dark. And when he was home, he hardly noticed Rosa. She longed for a smile or kind word from him. She longed, also, for Ma's return, not only for her own sake, but for Papa's too.

Unlike Papa, Mrs. Graziano was always happy to spend time with Rosa. When Rosa sat down for her after-school snack, Mrs. Graziano sat down too, and asked about Rosa's day. At supper, Mrs. Graziano often told Rosa about her own family and the latest antics of her grandchildren. But the best part of the day came in the evening, when they worked together on the puzzle. With

Gelsomino singing happily in the background, Rosa could forget her troubles for a while as she concentrated on the puzzle.

By Thursday evening, Rosa and Mrs. Graziano had already completed the bell tower, part of the Doge's Palace, and about a third of the canal. Mrs. Graziano quickly added a piece to the Palace while Rosa tried to fit an odd-shaped blue piece into the canal. As she worked, Rosa wondered if her parents had ever been to Venice. She could try asking Papa, but he probably wouldn't answer.

The blue piece didn't seem to fit anywhere. Rosa dropped it on the table and said, "Mrs. Graziano, why is Papa ignoring me?"

Mrs. Graziano turned to Rosa. "He does not talk to you?"

Rosa shook her head. "He hardly even looks at me. And when I ask about Ma, he just shrugs."

"Be patient with him, Rosa. I am sure he does not mean to hurt your feelings. All he can think about now is your mama."

"Ma's going to be okay, isn't she?"

"Of course she is." Mrs. Graziano set down the puzzle piece she'd been holding. "But your papa won't rest easy till she is home." Mrs. Graziano sighed. "You know, he reminds me of my Alberto, God rest his soul." She made a quick sign of the cross. "Alberto, he worked construction, too."

Rosa nodded. Mr. Graziano had helped Papa get a job once.

"Alberto was very good with his hands, like your papa. There was nothing my Alberto could not fix." Mrs. Graziano smiled. "But he had a hard time when I got sick. He wanted to fix me too, but that, he could not do."

"When were you sick?"

"Before you were born—about twelve years ago," Mrs. Graziano said. "I had cancer."

"Cancer!" Rosa said.

"It's all right." Mrs. Graziano patted Rosa's hand. "I am fine now. But for a while the doctors, they were not sure I would be okay. And Alberto, he was so worried, he almost forgot we had four children to take care of. When he was not at work, he was at *l'ospedale* with me, just like your papa is with your mama. Only I was there *due mesi.*"

"You were in the hospital two months! What did your kids do all that time?"

"My oldest, he took charge. Al was twenty then, and the other three were old enough to take care of themselves pretty good. My sister, she checked on them every day. She made sure they had plenty to eat. And if they needed something, Al, he found a way to get his papa's attention."

Mrs. Graziano took Rosa's hand in hers. "You have to do the same now, Rosa, until your mama comes home. Be *persistente.*"

"I'll try," Rosa answered. "But how long will it be before Ma comes home?"

"That is a good question for your papa."

Rosa decided to ask Papa that very night. When he sat down to eat supper, she sat down across from him. "Papa, there's something I need to know," she said quickly. "When is Ma coming home?"

"What?"

"When is Ma coming home?"

Papa shrugged and took a slice of bread from the basket.

"Please tell me, Papa," Rosa persisted. "She's been in the hospital eleven days now."

Finally, Papa said in a worn-out voice, "I don't know, Rosa." He tore his bread in two. "Another week. Maybe more."

"Another week? Why so long?"

"She is sick, Rosa." He dipped the bread into his stew. "These things take time." He went on eating in silence.

Rosa thought of what Mrs. Graziano had said—Papa's silence was because he was worried about Ma. Rosa hoped Ma would be home soon, so they could both stop worrying.

Another week went by. Then, on Friday, Papa came home earlier than usual. Mrs. Graziano and Rosa were doing dishes when he knocked at the back door. He walked in without waiting for an answer. "I have good news," Papa said, smiling for the first time in almost three weeks. "Frannie is coming home tomorrow."

"Hurray!" Rosa shouted, throwing her towel into the air. The towel landed on her head. Rosa laughed.

Mrs. Graziano laughed too. She took the towel from Rosa and dried her hands. "This is wonderful news, Giuseppe."

Rosa hugged Papa. "The very best news," she said. Now they could finally go back to the way things were before.

14

Broken Bubbles

SATURDAY MORNING, MRS. Graziano helped Rosa with the laundry. "Tell your papa not to worry about supper tonight," Mrs. Graziano said as they hung sheets on the backyard clothesline. "I am baking bread today. I will make a pizza for you and your papa, and soup for your mama."

"Thanks, Mrs. Graziano."

After Mrs. Graziano left, Rosa carried the empty laundry basket into the house. She cleaned the bathroom next. She wanted the house spotless for Ma.

When Papa came home from the grocery store, Rosa was sweeping the kitchen floor. She gave him Mrs. Graziano's message. "That's nice of her," he said, taking a carton of eggs from the grocery bag. "But starting tomorrow, *I* will do the cooking."

"I didn't know you could cook, Papa."

"Did you forget?" He held up his hands. "These hands are *straordinarie*."

Rosa laughed. Papa had never called his hands extraordinary before. He smiled, and Rosa noticed that the shadow had finally left his face.

She finished sweeping while Papa put away the rest of the groceries. Rosa was emptying the dustpan into the trash when he turned to her and said, "I'm going to get your mama now."

"How long will it take?" Rosa asked.

"About an hour. Will you be done then?"

Rosa nodded. "I just have to wash the kitchen floor and make the bed."

"That's my Rosalina." Papa ruffled Rosa's hair. "Your mama will not be able to do much for a while. She will need lots of help from you."

Rosa smiled. She planned to take care of Ma, just the way Ma had taken care of her when she'd had chicken pox. Rosa would bring her mother tea and read to her. And when it was time to sleep, Rosa would fluff Ma's pillow and make sure she had enough blankets.

After Papa left, Rosa filled a bucket with warm, soapy water. The suds reminded her of the bubble baths Ma used to give her. While Rosa played with the bubbles, Ma would wash her back and sing "Ave Maria." Just thinking of those baths left Rosa feeling warm all over.

Starting at the back door, Rosa scrubbed the faded yellow linoleum on her hands and knees, the way Ma had done on Rosa's birthday. Ma had looked so funny that morning—

Rosa had laughed at the way Ma's baby-filled belly practically touched the kitchen floor.

Picturing that scene now brought tears to Rosa's eyes. The empty-cave feeling came back so suddenly her chest hurt.

Rosa dropped her rag into the bucket. She had to keep busy or the emptiness might overpower her. She swallowed her tears and reached into the water for the rag. As she wrung it out, the splattering drops burst the last of the bubbles. She hurried to finish the floor.

Before putting the clean sheets on Ma's bed, Rosa dusted the bedroom furniture. She had to climb onto the bed to reach the wooden crucifix hanging above the headboard. She dusted the figure of Jesus on the cross, but avoided looking into his eyes. Rosa hadn't prayed since the day of Joseph's funeral.

Rosa carried the last of the chairs back to the kitchen. She glanced out the window just as Papa came out the side door of the garage. He stopped, turned, and reached back into the doorway. Then Ma stepped over the threshold, grabbing Papa for support. Ma was finally home!

But something was wrong. Leaning against Papa, Ma looked so small, almost shrunken. She took a tiny step toward the house.

Rosa hurried to the back porch. When she saw Ma's face, Rosa's heart stopped. Ma's skin was as white as the sheets Rosa had just put on the bed. And her eyes reminded Rosa of the charcoal in the grill after the fire had gone out.

Rosa took a breath, and her heart started again. She stepped out the door to watch Ma from the top of the stairs. Rosa's heart beat fast now, but the rest of her felt numb. What had they done to Ma?

Ma stared at the ground in front of her as she and Papa moved in slow motion toward the house. Still, she stumbled over a crack in the sidewalk. She clutched Papa's arm tighter, looking like a scared child. Rosa froze. She'd never seen Ma afraid.

"It's okay, Frannie," Papa said. "Take your time."

When Ma finally reached the stairs, she tilted her head back as if she were gazing up at a mountaintop. Rosa took a breath to calm herself. "Hi, Ma," she said, but her high-pitched voice sounded like it belonged to someone else. Rosa swallowed and tried again. "Welcome home."

Ma looked at Rosa. A spark of recognition flickered in her eyes, then they went blank again. Ma didn't move or speak. Rosa thought, *What's wrong with her?*

"Here, Frannie," Papa said, in the softest voice Rosa had ever heard him use. "I'll carry you." He lifted Ma into his arms and carried her upstairs. Rosa held the screen door open, then followed them into the house.

Papa didn't put Ma down till he reached their room, where he laid her on the bed. Rosa hung back, outside the bedroom door, dazed and confused.

Papa came over to her, pressed his finger to

his lips in a shushing signal, and started to shut the door.

"Wait," Rosa said, holding up her hand. "I want to be with Ma."

"Not now," Papa whispered. The shadow had returned to his face. "She needs to rest." He shut the door.

Rosa stood there, staring at the door, but seeing only Ma's empty eyes. The blood pounded in Rosa's throat. She wanted to bang on the door and say, "Let me in! I need to talk to Ma." Instead, she ran to her room.

She grabbed Lamby and buried her face in his softness. "Oh, Lamby," Rosa said, stroking his fur, "This is all my fault. If I hadn't prayed for a brother, Ma would never have gotten sick." Lamby was soon soaked in her tears.

Rosa patted Lamby dry with her sheet. Then she reached for Uncle Sal's handkerchief on the nightstand. Her hand brushed the necklace and cross she'd left there so long ago. After blowing her nose, Rosa picked up the necklace.

She stared at the gold cross. Rosa still didn't understand why God had let baby Joseph die, but God *had* answered her prayers for a brother. Maybe if she prayed for Ma, God would answer her prayers again.

Keeping her eyes on the cross, Rosa said, "Dear God, I'm sorry I stopped praying." Rosa swallowed. "I'm sorry, too, for getting mad at you." The cross blurred as Rosa's eyes filled with tears again. "If you'll help Ma get well, I promise to never stop praying again. And I'll be extra good from now on."

Rosa put on her necklace. Then she knelt beside her bed, folded her hands together, and started to pray.

15 ❧

Green Soup

THE NEXT MORNING, Rosa woke to the smell of burned toast, just as she had the day Ma went into the hospital. *Ma!* Rosa jumped out of bed.

But instead of Mrs. Graziano, Papa was in the kitchen this time. He stood at the counter, his back to Rosa, cursing in Italian as he tried to pry a slice of bread from the toaster. Rosa sneaked down the hall to his bedroom.

From the doorway, Rosa saw Ma lying in bed, asleep. Except for the gray circles under her eyes, Ma's skin was still ghostly white. Rosa stepped closer and listened for Ma's breathing — faint but steady.

Back in the kitchen, Papa finally pulled the burned toast from the toaster. He'd obviously cut Mrs. Graziano's homemade bread too thick.

"Can I help?" Rosa asked.

Papa looked up. "Rosa. I didn't hear you." He dropped the toast into the garbage pail, then brushed black crumbs from his hands. "Yes, I could use some help. I want to make a special breakfast for your mama. One she will not refuse." The night before, Papa had tried to feed Ma some of Mrs. Graziano's soup, but she wouldn't eat.

He reached for the loaf of bread. "If I cut more bread, will you toast it?"

"Sure."

Papa sliced the bread thinner this time. While Rosa watched the toaster, he poured olive oil into a skillet and began chopping an onion.

The toast popped up with a loud *ching*. Rosa spread butter over the hot bread, smoothing out the lumps. Her stomach grumbled. She had been too worried about Ma to eat much of Mrs. Graziano's pizza the night before. Now Rosa's stomach would have to wait till she'd finished helping Papa.

The smell of raw onion made Rosa's eyes smart. The odor must have bothered Papa, too, because he sniffled several times. He stepped away from the counter and stared up at the ceiling. Rosa wondered what he was looking at, then realized he was blinking hard to hold back tears. Papa never cried. He blew his nose in his handkerchief, then finished chopping without a single tear slipping down his cheek.

The oil sizzled and splattered as Papa dropped the onions into the skillet. He quickly turned down the gas and began stirring. The aroma of onions frying soon replaced the burned-toast smell. As Papa worked, his shoulders relaxed. When he spoke again, he sounded almost cheerful. "Get me the eggs, Rosa."

Rosa set the egg carton on the counter. "Papa," she said. "Is Ma going to be okay?"

Papa cracked one of the eggs into a bowl. "Yes," he said, but his voice wasn't as confident as Rosa would have liked. "The doctor said she has to get lots of rest and eat well. You and me, we have to make sure she does that, okay?"

Rosa nodded. She thought of what Mrs. Graziano had said about Papa being like Mr. Graziano and needing to fix things. Maybe together she and Papa could "fix" Ma. They'd start by serving her a breakfast fit for a queen.

Rosa took out Ma's best serving plate — the one with a grapevine painted along the edge. Tiny clusters of purple grapes dotted the grapevine's green leaves. Rosa set the plate next to the stove for the eggs. Then she sliced fresh strawberries and a banana into a bowl, arranging the fruit so it looked like the picture she'd seen on a magazine in the supermarket checkout. As she put the bowl on Ma's silver serving tray, Rosa's stomach growled again.

After Papa slid the egg-and-onion *frittata* onto the grapevine plate, Rosa arranged the four toast halves around it. Papa placed the plate on the tray while Rosa poured a glass of orange juice. Finally, she added a napkin and silverware to the tray.

"Bellissimo." Papa grinned as he wrapped his big, strong hands around the silver tray's delicate handles. Standing so proud and tall, he reminded Rosa of one of those fancy butlers in the movies.

Rosa looked at the colorful tray, and her chest filled with pride. She couldn't help grinning, too.

She followed Papa to the bedroom. *"Buon giorno, signora,"* he said as he entered the room. "Good day, my lady."

Rosa covered her mouth to keep from giggling. Papa even sounded like a butler.

In a deep voice, Papa said, "I have brought

your breakfast, *signora.*" Ma rolled onto her back, but she didn't say anything. From the foot of the bed, Rosa could see that Ma's eyes were still closed.

Papa nodded toward Rosa, signaling for her to take the tray. Rosa leaned the tray against the triple dresser.

Papa walked to Ma's side of the bed and nudged her shoulder. "Frannie, wake up," he said, speaking softly now. "Rosa and I made breakfast for you."

"I don't want anything," Ma said.

"We prepared a special *colazione.*" He pointed at the tray. "Look."

Ma opened her eyes. "I don't want it," she said.

"But Frannie, you need to eat to get strong."

She rolled away from Papa. "Leave me be."

Papa looked at Rosa, his face sad and confused at the same time. He nodded toward the tray. "You better take it away."

Rosa glanced at Ma.

"Rosa." Papa waved her away.

She carried the tray to the kitchen and set it on the counter. They had failed. Now what?

As Rosa stood staring at the tray, she heard the Collettis from upstairs thump down the back steps. She suddenly remembered it was Sunday. Rosa had already missed Mass two Sundays in a row, for no good reason. How could she expect God to answer her prayers when she ignored her Sunday obligation?

Rosa looked up at the clock. If she hurried, she could still make nine o'clock Mass. She ran to her room, dressed quickly, said good-bye to Papa, then rushed out the door.

On the way to church, Rosa's stomach reminded her again that she hadn't eaten breakfast. This time, she offered up her hunger for Ma. Rosa prayed her sacrifice would bring back Ma's appetite.

That afternoon, Uncle Sal and Aunt Ida came over. When Rosa opened the door, Uncle Sal was holding a large cast-iron pot. From behind him, Aunt Ida said, "Out of the way, Rosa. The pot is heavy."

Rosa stepped back.

Papa greeted his aunt and uncle in the kitchen. "Thanks for coming," he said.

Uncle Sal set the pot on the stove, then shook Papa's hand.

"I don't know what to do," Papa said. "She won't eat."

"She has eaten nothing?" Aunt Ida asked.

Papa turned to Aunt Ida. "All she's had is water."

Aunt Ida turned on the gas under the pot. "Let me see if she will take some soup."

"Mrs. Graziano made *pastina* yesterday," Rosa said, "but Ma wouldn't eat it."

"Ah, but I made *scarola in brodo*," Aunt Ida said.

Rosa wondered if Aunt Ida knew escarole soup was Ma's favorite, and Rosa's, too.

Aunt Ida lifted the pot lid to stir the soup.

Rosa had to admit that it smelled even better than Mrs. Graziano's *pastina*. "*Scarola* has lots of iron," Aunt Ida said. "Good for the blood."

"Sit down, Uncle Sal," Papa said. "Can I get you something to drink?"

"Never mind me." Uncle Sal pulled out a chair. "I am here to help *you*."

Papa sat down next to his uncle.

When the soup was hot, Aunt Ida ladled the dark green concoction into a bowl. Rosa started to follow her to Ma's room, but then she heard a strange sound, like a stifled sob. Rosa stopped in the hall and turned around to see Papa sitting hunched over the kitchen table with his head in his hands.

Uncle Sal put a hand on Papa's shoulder. "I know, these are hard times for you, Giuseppe," Uncle Sal said in Italian, "but Francesca is strong. I'm sure she'll be okay."

Papa raised his head. "I want to believe that."

Rosa crept closer, till she stood beside the fridge. The refrigerator motor rumbled in her left ear as Papa went on, speaking Italian now, too. "On top of everything else, my boss is mad because I asked for more time off to take care of Frannie. He said that if the job falls behind schedule, he'll replace me with another bricklayer." Papa shook his head. "I can't leave Frannie like this." He waved his hand toward Ma's bedroom.

Rosa pressed closer to the fridge so Papa wouldn't notice her. The cool metal trembled against her skin.

Papa shook his head again. "If I stay home, I'll lose my job."

"You don't have to worry about Francesca," Uncle Sal said. "Ida and I can come over during the day while you are at work."

"But I leave so early," Papa said. "I hate to put you to so much trouble."

"Trouble? There is no such thing as trouble among family." Uncle Sal patted Papa's back. "Did you forget we were farmers in the Old Country? We're used to getting up early."

"*Grazie,*" Papa said.

"You're welcome," Uncle Sal said, speaking English again. "Now that's settled, maybe I'll have that drink."

Rosa turned and hurried down the hall.

She could hardly believe what she saw when she reached Ma's room: Ma sitting up in bed with her mouth open, like a baby bird waiting to be fed. Rosa watched as Aunt Ida spooned soup into Ma's mouth. Rosa smiled. God had answered her prayers!

Rosa stayed in the doorway, afraid Aunt Ida's spell would break if she walked into the room. When Ma had finished, Aunt Ida pulled the coverlet over her. "Rest now, Francesca. Later, I will bring you a nice cup of tea."

Aunt Ida shut the bedroom door and grinned at Rosa, obviously proud of herself. Rosa asked, "How did you do that?"

Aunt Ida whispered, "We women have our ways."

Rosa felt her face flush. Why did Aunt Ida always try to make her feel like a baby?

In the kitchen, Papa's eyebrows went up when he saw the empty bowl. "You got her to eat?"

Aunt Ida nodded. Papa grabbed her in a bear hug. He lifted Aunt Ida so far off the floor her pointy black shoes looked as though they'd slide right off her feet.

"Put me down, Giuseppe," Aunt Ida said, laughing. "Or you will need a nurse, too."

Uncle Sal joined in the laughter.

Rosa stood next to the fridge with her mouth shut tight. Even though she felt grateful that God had answered her prayers for her mother, Rosa had wanted to be the one to take care of Ma.

Aunt Ida went to the stove and stirred the soup with the ladle. "There's plenty more," she said. "Would you like some, Rosa?"

Rosa shook her head. She didn't want any of *her* soup.

16

Twelve Seedlings

"TIME TO GET ready for school," Uncle Sal said as he gently prodded Rosa awake the next day.

Rosa rubbed the sleep from her eyes. "Do I have to go? Can't I stay home and help take care of Ma?"

"Do not worry," Uncle Sal said. "Ida and I will take very good care of your mama."

Rosa didn't like leaving Aunt Ida in charge, but she had no choice.

After getting dressed, Rosa went into the

kitchen. She had just finished her cereal when Aunt Ida came in carrying a bundle of sheets.

"Are those Ma's sheets?" Rosa asked.

Aunt Ida nodded. "Do you know where she keeps her laundry basket? I looked everywhere for it."

"It's in the basement, next to the washer." Rosa almost added, "Where I left it," but instead she said, "I just changed Ma's sheets. The day she came home."

"Two days ago? A sick person needs clean linens every day." Aunt Ida's face softened as she said, "Of course, child, *you* wouldn't know that."

Rosa felt the blood rise to her ears. She hated when Aunt Ida talked to her that way. Rosa got up and put her breakfast things in the sink.

While Aunt Ida was in the basement, Rosa tiptoed to the dining room. Uncle Sal sat in the living room, reading *Il Progresso*, the Italian newspaper. Rosa ducked into Ma's room.

Ma lay on her back with her head turned

161

toward the dresser, her face as pale as ever. The curves of her colorless lips sagged, making her look sad. Rosa wondered how Ma felt inside. Did she have the empty-cave feeling, too? Ma hadn't gone to the baby's funeral either. But she must have seen him, maybe even held him in her arms. When Ma was well again, she could tell Rosa what Joseph had looked like. The thought lightened Rosa's heart.

She stepped closer. Aunt Ida had managed to get Ma to eat again, but maybe what Ma really needed was to be cheered up. To forget about the empty cave for a while. Rosa whispered, "Hi, Ma. How're you today?"

Keeping her eyes closed, Ma raised her hand. Was it a wave, or a sign to go away? Rosa didn't know. Before she could find out, she heard footsteps. Rosa hurried from the room, but it was too late. Aunt Ida was standing outside the door.

Aunt Ida spoke in a high-pitched whisper. "What were you doing?"

"Saying goodbye to Ma."

"And that was more important than letting her rest?"

Rosa wanted to explain about trying to cheer Ma up, but Aunt Ida didn't give her a chance. "You better go *now*, Rosa."

Rosa grabbed her school things and ran outside. Keeping her promise to God about being good was going to be awfully hard with Aunt Ida around.

When Rosa got home from school, Uncle Sal was parking his Buick in front of her house. "Ah, Rosa, you are home," he said as he walked around the car. "Just in time to help with the *sorpresa*."

"What surprise?"

Uncle Sal opened the passenger door of the car. A box of seedlings sat on the floor of the front seat. "I noticed your papa has not put in any tomatoes or peppers yet." He pointed at the seedlings. "I thought you could help me plant these. It would be a nice *sorpresa*, no?"

"Yes," Rosa answered. Earlier that spring, Ma and Rosa had planted seeds in one of their two garden strips in the backyard. But the larger plot still lay empty. Maybe Uncle Sal's surprise would help cheer Ma up.

Uncle Sal said, "I'll carry these out back while you change."

Rosa ran ahead. But when she burst through the back door, Aunt Ida was sitting at the kitchen table mending one of Papa's work socks. She frowned at Rosa. "Hush, child! Did you forget your mama is sick?"

Rosa didn't see how she could be bothering her mother when Ma wasn't even in the room. Instead of saying so, though, Rosa asked, "How is she?"

"Still very weak. And tired."

"Can I see her?"

Aunt Ida put one last stitch in the sock. "Not now," she said. "I just looked in on her." Aunt Ida bent over and, using her teeth, snipped the long gray thread from the sock. "She's asleep."

Asleep again? When would Ma get out of bed?

Rosa quickly changed into play clothes, drank a glass of milk, and joined Uncle Sal in the backyard. The box of vegetable seedlings sat in the shade of the garage. Uncle Sal stood over the empty plot alongside the Fitzhughs' chainlink fence. "Looks like your papa already worked the soil."

Rosa pointed at the small garden on the opposite side, next to Mrs. Graziano's fence. Tiny green shoots dotted the dirt. "I helped Ma plant seeds over there," Rosa said. "I think the lettuce and peas are coming up already."

Uncle Sal walked over and examined the leaves. "Yes, they are," he said. "And radishes, too. They need a good watering. We will do that later. First, where does your papa keep his spade?"

Uncle Sal dug a row alongside the Fitzhughs' fence, then mixed in some fertilizer. When he'd finished, he leaned the spade against the chainlink fence, took off his straw hat, and wiped the sweat from his forehead with his handkerchief. "The sun, it is hot," he said, then put his hat back on.

Uncle Sal took two tomato seedlings from the box in the shade. He handed one to Rosa. "Keep your fingers flat on the dirt, supporting the stem," he told her. "Then turn the pot over, like this." He flipped the plant upside down so that the drainage holes faced up. "Give the bottom of the pot a tap. When you pull on the pot, the plant should slide out." Uncle Sal patted the base of the pot, then tugged it off. Sure enough, the square of roots and dirt stayed in his hand.

Rosa turned over her seedling and imitated what Uncle Sal had done. The pot slipped off easily. "Like this?" Rosa raised the plant toward Uncle Sal.

Uncle Sal smiled. "Very good." He carefully turned his seedling right side up and placed it at the head of the row he'd dug. "Put yours there," he said, pointing to a spot about two feet away.

After they had set all six tomato plants in the ground, Uncle Sal showed Rosa how to fill in the dirt and pat it down so that the seedlings stood straight. She liked the feel of the warm, dry dirt between her fingers, and the smell of the fresh green plants. But most of all, she liked seeing the baby plants all lined up in a neat row.

Uncle Sal dug another row parallel to the first. When they'd finished planting the green-pepper seedlings, Rosa stood and brushed the dirt from her hands.

"You are a natural-born farmer, Rosa." Uncle Sal squeezed her arm. "It must be in your blood."

Rosa smiled down at the two rows of seedlings. She looked forward to watching the tiny plants grow. And to showing them to Ma soon.

17 ❧

Magic Medicine

AT THE START of Wednesday's spelling lesson, Sister Ambrose announced, "One week from today, we'll have our class spelling bee. Our two best spellers will go on to the school competition on Thursday, June first." Sister began passing out papers. "Here is your word list. Please review the words in your spelling books, too."

Rosa could feel AnnaMaria watching her. When Rosa had placed third in the class bee last year, AnnaMaria had said, "You'll do better next time." Now next time was here. But how could Rosa win the competition without Ma's help?

After school, Rosa repeated her routine of waiting in the bathroom until AnnaMaria and the other kids had left. This time, though, when Rosa finally went outside, AnnaMaria was standing at the corner talking to Bridget Sullivan. Rosa looked around for a place to hide, then ducked behind the tall bushes surrounding the rectory's meditation garden.

Inside the garden, Rosa sat down on the concrete bench facing the statue of Saint Francis of Assisi. To her right, two blackbirds were fighting at the wooden bird feeder. Below them, sparrows pecked at the seeds the bigger birds scattered. One small, light-colored sparrow searched for seed far from the others, near the feet of Saint Francis. Every so often the lone bird cocked her head toward the other sparrows. She looked as though she couldn't decide whether to join them.

Absorbed in watching the birds, Rosa

didn't notice AnnaMaria slip into the garden. When AnnaMaria said, "Hi," Rosa jumped up in surprise. The startled birds took off.

"Sorry," AnnaMaria said. "I didn't mean to scare you. What're you doing?"

"Watching the birds." Rosa sat back down.

AnnaMaria sat next to her. "I want to ask you something, Rosa."

Rosa stared at the feeder. She hoped AnnaMaria's question wouldn't be: "Why are you avoiding me?"

"I was wondering," AnnaMaria said, "if you'd help me study for the bee."

Rosa turned to AnnaMaria. "You want my help?"

AnnaMaria nodded. "I don't expect to win, or anything like that. I just don't want to be the first one out again, like last year."

Rosa didn't know that being eliminated early had bothered AnnaMaria that much. "I thought Jimmy Nelson was the first one out."

"Yeah, but he doesn't count." AnnaMaria giggled.

Rosa giggled, too.

"So what do you say?" AnnaMaria asked.

Rosa hated to say no to her friend, but she couldn't imagine going to AnnaMaria's house with Antonio there. "Can't your mother help you?"

"Well, she's kind of busy with Anto—" AnnaMaria blushed as she caught herself, then said, "Mom has lots to do these days. Couldn't we study at your house?"

That would solve the problem of Antonio, but Rosa didn't know if Aunt Ida would allow it. "I'll have to see if it's okay," Rosa said.

When Rosa reached home, she saw Mrs. Graziano working in her garden. Mrs. Graziano had the only house in the neighborhood with a flower garden for a front yard. "*Ciao*, Rosa," Mrs. Graziano said, getting up from her knees. "How are you doing?"

"I'm okay," Rosa said.

Mrs. Graziano walked over to the fence. "I miss you."

Rosa thought of their after-school talks. The only time Aunt Ida talked to Rosa was to scold her. "I miss you, too, Mrs. Graziano."

"How's your mama?" Mrs. Graziano asked.

Rosa shrugged. She didn't want to tell Mrs. Graziano about Ma staying in bed all the time. Instead, she said, "How're your grandchildren?"

"They grow like *erbacce*." Mrs. Graziano pointed at the pile of weeds she'd pulled from her flower bed. "Next week, my daughter, she goes back to work part-time. I will be babysitter for her *bambini*." Mrs. Graziano grinned.

"They're lucky to have you," Rosa said. *Very* lucky, she thought. "I better go in now."

"Say hello to your mama from me."

Rosa walked into the kitchen to find Ma sitting at the table.

"Ma!" Rosa dropped her books onto the closest chair. "You're out of bed."

Ma turned toward Rosa, but her eyes looked dull.

Aunt Ida carried a saucepan to the table.

Rosa knew from the sweet smell that it held chamomile tea. "The doctor came by this afternoon," Aunt Ida said. She poured the pale tea through a wire mesh strainer to remove the chamomile blossoms. "He wants your mama to get out of bed for a little while every day. He said she will never get strong if all she does is lie around."

Aunt Ida made Ma sound lazy, not sick. Rosa wished her godmother could be more like Mrs. Graziano.

Rosa said to Ma, "You must be getting better." Ma didn't look any better, though. Her red flannel robe made her pale face seem grayer than ever. Rosa kissed Ma's cheek. It felt cold.

"Guess what, Ma?" Rosa said. "Next week's the spelling bee. Do you think you could quiz me on my words again, like you did last year?"

"Humph," Aunt Ida grunted, as though she thought Rosa had asked the impossible. At least Aunt Ida didn't say anything this time.

Rosa watched Ma's face and waited for her

answer. Studying together would be good for both of them. It would give Ma something to do.

But Ma shook her head, saying quietly, "I'm too tired, Rosa." She stared at the steaming cup of tea.

Rosa stirred the hot liquid, then scooped a spoonful and blew on it. Maybe she could spoon-feed Ma the same way Aunt Ida had done with the escarole soup. Raising the spoon, Rosa said, "Ready?"

Ma nodded.

As Rosa tipped the tea into her mother's mouth, she thought of how Ma called chamomile tea "magic medicine." Whenever Rosa was sick, it didn't matter what she had, Ma always nursed her back to health with chamomile tea. Now Rosa could do the same for her.

After only a few spoonfuls, though, Ma's face flushed red. Beads of sweat broke out on her forehead and cheeks.

"Aunt Ida, something's wrong," Rosa said. "Ma's sweating like crazy."

Aunt Ida loosened Ma's robe and slipped it from her shoulders. "Francesca, you're soaking wet," Aunt Ida said. "I'll have to change your nightgown again."

"What is it?" Rosa asked. "Does she have a fever?"

Aunt Ida shook her head. "No. It's just the aftereffect of the surgery. The doctor said the new medicine will take care of it. Salvatore is out filling the prescription now." Aunt Ida put her hands under Ma's arm. "Come on, Francesca. Let's go back to your room." Aunt Ida tilted her head toward Ma's other side, a sign for Rosa to help. Together, they walked Ma to her bedroom, but Ma hardly leaned on them. Rosa sensed that Ma could walk without their help if she tried. Was the empty-cave feeling keeping her from trying?

Rosa returned to the kitchen. Not only had the magic medicine failed, it had made Ma worse. Rosa wondered if the doctor's medicine would work any better.

She carried her books to her room and pulled out the new spelling word list. Sitting on the bed, Rosa remembered the day a year ago when she'd first told Ma about the spelling bee.

That day, Rosa came home to find Ma working at her sewing machine. As soon as Rosa explained the competition, Ma turned from the machine and said, "I will help you study. It will be good practice for my English."

"But Ma, you talk fine," Rosa said.

"Talking is one thing," Ma said, "reading is another." Even though Ma had gone to "English school" when she first came to America, she still had trouble reading English.

Ma stood up. "Did they tell you what words to study?"

Rosa wished she hadn't mentioned the competition. She hated spelling. But it was too late now. She handed Ma the word list, then sat down at the dining-room table and pushed a dress pattern out of her way. With her elbows on the table, Rosa rested her head in her hands. It was going to be a long afternoon.

But the spelling practice soon turned into a game — a guessing game. The first word Ma called out was "ah-eez-lay."

Rosa had never heard of "ah-eez-lay." Ma had to be saying the word wrong. Rosa resisted the urge to look at the spelling list — she wanted to figure it out for herself. She thought about the rules for pronouncing Italian words. "I know," she said, jumping up. "The word is *aisle*."

"Aisle?" Ma said. "What the bride walks down to get married in church?"

Rosa nodded, covering her mouth so she wouldn't laugh at Ma's confused look.

Ma pointed at the list. "How can this word be *aisle*? There are too many letters."

"Is it spelled A-I-S-L-E?"

"Exactly," Ma said.

"That's *aisle*."

"This language is so strange." Ma shook her head. "What's this next word, then?" Her forehead wrinkled as she sounded out, "Ahn-chee-aint."

Rosa was quicker this time. "That must be *ancient*."

"Ancient?"

Ma looked so puzzled Rosa couldn't help smiling. Ma held the list toward Rosa. "Why do they put in so many letters you do not say?"

Rosa shrugged. "I don't know. But it sure makes spelling hard."

Ma's eyes brightened. She patted Rosa's shoulder. "Do not worry, Rosa. When we are finished, you will say spelling is easy."

"Easy," Rosa repeated. Then, trying to look serious, she sat up tall and said, "E-A-S-Y."

"No!" Ma said, exaggerating her surprise this time. "Really?"

Rosa laughed. "Yes."

"Give me your *penna*." Ma took Rosa's pen and added *easy* to the list.

By the day of the competition, spelling

really was easy. Ma's funny pronunciations helped Rosa remember how to spell the words with silent letters. That day, Rosa amazed everyone by coming in third. If she hadn't forgotten the second *m* in *accommodate*, she would have gone on to represent the class in the all-school spelling bee.

"*Brava*, Rosa!" Ma said when Rosa told her the news after school. "I am so proud of you."

"But I wasn't good enough to make the school competition." Rosa stared at the yellow linoleum of the kitchen floor. She had let Ma down.

Ma lifted Rosa's chin with her hand. Looking right into Rosa's eyes, she said, "You are much better than 'good enough,' Rosa." The gold flecks of light in Ma's hazel eyes melted Rosa's disappointment. "You know," Ma said, "in the Olympics, they give a bronze medal to the athlete who comes in third place. It is a great *onore*."

Now, sitting on her bed, Rosa smiled at the memory. The flecks of gold that had glittered in Ma's eyes that day had been worth more to Rosa than any bronze medal. She missed seeing that light in Ma's eyes.

Staring down at this year's word list, Rosa got an idea. Maybe if she won the spelling bee this time, the light would come back to Ma's eyes. That could be the magic medicine that finally made Ma better.

Studying together could help both AnnaMaria and Rosa get what they wanted. Rosa reached for the cross around her neck and prayed Aunt Ida would let her friend come over.

18 ❧

Old Photographs

AT BREAKFAST ON Thursday, Rosa asked
Aunt Ida, "Can AnnaMaria come over after
school to study for the spelling bee?"

"That's fine," Aunt Ida said, getting up
from the table. Then she stopped and added,
"As long as you stay on the back porch and do
not disturb your mama."

Rosa looked down at her bowl of cereal. She
didn't need to be reminded not to bother Ma.

• • •

On the way home from school, Rosa warned AnnaMaria, "We can't make too much noise or Aunt Ida won't let you stay. She's a real witch."

When Rosa opened the back door, she was surprised to see that Aunt Ida had swept out the porch and set up a card table in the corner. She'd left a plate of homemade cookies, too. As Rosa and AnnaMaria put down their things, Aunt Ida came out and asked, "Would you girls like milk with your *pizzelle*, or lemonade?"

"Milk, please," AnnaMaria said.

Rosa nodded, too stunned to talk.

AnnaMaria bit into one of the thin waffle cookies and whispered, "She doesn't seem like a witch."

"You don't know her like I do."

Aunt Ida was just as nice during their Friday afternoon study session. And when Rosa asked if AnnaMaria could come back Saturday, Aunt Ida said, "Why don't you invite your friend for lunch? Your papa will be working, and Salvatore has some things to do at home."

Aunt Ida was obviously trying to impress AnnaMaria, and that was fine by Rosa. At least with her friend around, Rosa could forget for a while that Ma was still sick and that Papa was hardly ever home.

On Sunday, Uncle Sal and Aunt Ida stayed away, leaving Papa and Rosa to care for Ma on their own. Aunt Ida had left a lasagna, though, so they didn't have to cook. At lunchtime, Rosa placed the pan in the oven and set the table.

"Smells good," Papa said, coming into the kitchen. "Is it almost done?"

"Five more minutes," Rosa answered. She could hardly wait—the lasagna really did smell delicious.

Papa smiled. "I will get your mama."

When he came back a few minutes later, his smile was gone. "She's not hungry." He sat down at the table. "Maybe she'll eat something later."

Steam rose from the lasagna as Papa placed a large slice on Rosa's plate. She waited for him to say grace, but he started eating without a word. Not even his usual *"Buon appetito!"* — the Italian version of "Dig in."

Melted cheese oozed onto Rosa's plate as she cut into her lasagna. If only she knew her godmother's secret for getting Ma out of bed. Ma had been coming to the table for lunch and dinner the past three days. But Papa didn't know that — he hadn't been home for supper all week.

While Rosa poked at the bits of ground beef in her lasagna, Papa ate heartily. Except for the scraping of Papa's fork against his plate, the only sound in the kitchen was the *tick-tick-tick* of the wall clock. Meals were never this quiet when Uncle Sal was around. Rosa missed her godfather.

The thought made her feel guilty. Rosa had hardly seen Papa since the Sunday before.

"It sure is nice out," Rosa said. "Maybe we could play catch later."

Papa shook his head. "Not today, Rosa. I am tired." He poured more wine into his glass. "Why don't we watch the game together instead? The Cubs are playing the Cardinals."

"Sure, Papa." Of course he was tired. Papa had worked overtime every day this week, including Saturday. But she still felt disappointed.

Papa saw less than two innings of the Cubs game before falling asleep on the couch. The scoreless game bored Rosa, too. Her eyes soon grew heavy. She shook herself awake and went to check on Ma.

To her surprise, Rosa found Ma sitting up in bed, staring at the photographs on the triple dresser.

"Hi, Ma," Rosa said. "Are you hungry yet?"

Ma shook her head. "I would like some water, though." She pointed at the empty pitcher on the nightstand.

Rosa refilled the pitcher in the kitchen, then came back and poured water into Ma's glass. Ma took a long drink.

"Do you want to walk around a little?" Rosa asked. "I'll help you."

"Not now." Ma handed the glass to Rosa. "Maybe later."

After setting the glass down, Rosa glanced at the row of framed photographs on the dresser. Most of the pictures were old black-and-white ones taken in Italy — Ma walking through her village with a huge water urn on her head, Papa riding what looked like a miniature motorcycle, and Ma and Papa leaving the church on their wedding day. The only color picture was of Rosa in her First Communion dress, a big smile on her face. Happiness shone from her hazel eyes. Seeing the picture reminded Rosa of what Ma had told her, that she'd been born with blue eyes.

Still facing the dresser, Rosa said, "Remember the picture you showed me, Ma? The one where I was a baby in the bassinet with Lamby?"

When Ma didn't answer, Rosa turned around.

Ma nodded slowly. "I remember."

"Is that what baby Joseph looked like? Did he have blue eyes and lots of hair too?"

Ma shut her eyes and leaned into the wall above her headboard.

Rosa shouldn't have asked—it was too soon. "I'm sorry, Ma," Rosa said. "You don't have to tell me."

"I can't tell you." Ma opened her eyes, but she didn't look at Rosa. Instead, she stared at the lace curtains covering the window. "I don't know."

"You don't know?" Rosa's knees went weak. She moved to the bed and sat down.

Ma shrugged and said matter-of-factly, "I never saw him."

How could she say it like that, without any feeling? Didn't she need to know what Joseph had looked like, the way Rosa did?

Ma went on staring at the curtains. "The labor pain, it was *terribile*," she said. "The doctor put me to sleep." Ma's voice sounded hollow and distant, as though she were talking about some stranger. "I didn't wake up for two days. The baby was gone. And I was still in pain."

A horrible feeling crept into Rosa's stomach. The same feeling she'd had last Fourth of July at the beach, when Ma explained why she hadn't had more kids.

"I'm sorry, Ma." Tears trickled down Rosa's cheeks. "You don't hate me, do you?"

Ma turned to Rosa, a puzzled look on her face. "Why would I hate you?"

"It's all my fault. I prayed for God to send a baby."

"I don't blame you." Ma waved her hand, brushing away Rosa's words. "It was *destino*. I was never meant to have more children."

"Oh, Ma." Rosa hugged her mother.

Ma held Rosa awkwardly for a moment, as though she'd forgotten how to hug. She soon let go. That's when Rosa saw that her mother's cheek was wet. But it was from Rosa's tears. Ma's eyes were still dry.

Ma rubbed away the wet spot and lay down again. "I'm tired, Rosa."

188

In the living room, Rosa watched Papa sleeping on the couch. Had he seen baby Joseph? Maybe someday she could ask him, but not now.

She wandered out to the backyard. It was colder outside than she'd expected. She shivered despite the bright sunshine.

Rosa walked over to the vegetable garden. The seedlings didn't look any bigger than the day she and Uncle Sal had planted them, almost a week ago. Were the plants going to die, too?

As Rosa stared down at the seedlings, the empty-cave feeling came back stronger than ever. It felt like a huge hole in her chest — a hole she didn't know how to fill.

On her way back inside, Rosa noticed her spelling book on the porch table. She must have left it there after practicing with AnnaMaria the day before. Rosa picked up the book, but she didn't feel much like studying.

She thought of what Ma had said about

destiny. If there really was some power that controlled everything that happened, then it didn't matter if Rosa studied. Destiny had already decided the winner.

"That can't be," Rosa said out loud. How she did in the competition *had* to depend on how well she prepared. Maybe destiny controlled some things, but it didn't control everything. And she would prove it by winning the bee.

19 🌹

Holy Ground

ANNAMARIA HAD a dentist's appointment after school on Monday, so Rosa studied her spelling words alone. After a while, she took a break and went outside to help Uncle Sal in the garden.

Uncle Sal was connecting the hose to the water spigot. As he turned on the water he said, "You know, tomorrow is Memorial Day, Rosa."

"I know," Rosa answered. "There's no school." She picked up the end of the hose and rotated the nozzle till a fine spray showered the lettuce and pea plants. The sunlight filtering through the spray created a rainbow in midair.

Uncle Sal cleared his throat. "Tomorrow I go to *camposanto*. You want to come with me?"

Camposanto. The word meant holy ground. "You mean the cemetery?"

Uncle Sal nodded. "Your papa, he will not go. And your mama, she cannot go." He bent down to pull a weed from among the green pepper seedlings. "Someone should put flowers on the baby's grave."

The baby's grave. A chance to be close to her brother. That felt more important than ever—Rosa might never know now what Joseph had looked like. She aimed the hose higher. The rainbow's arc shimmered over the whole garden. "I'll come with you," she said.

The next day, Uncle Sal and Rosa stopped at the florist on the way to the cemetery. Rosa picked out a large pot of red geraniums. "Good choice," Uncle Sal said. Then he surprised her by buying a second, matching pot.

Rosa had never been to a cemetery. In the movies, cemeteries were creepy places people always avoided. Yet Rosa and Uncle Sal had to wait in a long line of cars to get into the cemetery where Joseph was buried.

"Everyone comes on Memorial Day," Uncle Sal explained. Everyone except Ma, Papa, and Aunt Ida, Rosa thought. She was glad it was just her and Uncle Sal, but she wondered why Aunt Ida hadn't come.

As the car inched closer to the cemetery entrance, Rosa looked through the chainlink fence at all the tombstones. They ranged in size from small rectangular stones to giant columns. Some even had crosses or statues of saints on top. The rows of tombstones reminded Rosa of soldiers silently guarding the graves. She wondered which one watched over Joseph.

Tiny American flags stood beside many of the tombstones, fluttering their red, white, and blue next to clusters of yellow and orange flowers. Rosa hadn't expected so much color. She'd always thought of cemeteries as gloomy places.

Inside the cemetery, Uncle Sal parked near a large white statue of Our Lady of Lourdes. Rosa knew the Blessed Mother had appeared to Saint Bernadette in Lourdes, France, a long time ago. Ever since then, people who visited Lourdes were often miraculously healed. Rosa wondered if Our Lady of Lourdes could help Ma.

Uncle Sal took one of the flower pots from the back seat. "Come, Rosa."

"Should I bring the other plant?"

He shook his head. "I have to do something before we go to the baby's grave."

Rosa followed Uncle Sal across the field of graves. Up close, she could see that the tombstones weren't all gray, as they had seemed from the road. Some were shades of brown, and even pink. Uncle Sal stopped at a grave near a huge maple tree. The grave's rectangular tombstone shone red-violet in the morning sun. Rosa read the writing carved into the stone:

SOFIA MARIA BERNARDI
March 10, 1899 — December 15, 1918

Rosa blinked, then read the name again. Who could she be? No one in the family had ever said anything about a Sofia Bernardi. Rosa turned to Uncle Sal. "Who was she?"

Uncle Sal got down on one knee and placed the pot of geraniums in the holder at the base of the tombstone. "My wife."

"Your wife? But Aunt Ida's your wife."

Uncle Sal leaned on the tombstone to pull himself back to a stand. He took off his straw hat and wiped his forehead with his handkerchief. "Sofia was my *first* wife. We were married only six months before she died."

How could it be? Uncle Sal married to someone else? Why hadn't he mentioned Sofia before?

Uncle Sal stared at the tombstone with his hat in his hand. His face softened. He looked almost happy.

Confused, Rosa asked, "How did she die?"

"Influenza. That year, there was an influenza *terribile*. Sofia, she was a little woman, like your mama, only not so strong. I called her *la mia uccellina*." Uncle Sal smiled. "My little bird."

Rosa thought of Aunt Ida—she couldn't imagine Uncle Sal ever calling her his little bird.

He turned toward the maple tree. "That tree was small when I picked this spot for Sofia. Not much bigger than you." He held his hand out even with the top of Rosa's head. "Now it gives shade to my *uccellina*, and it is a home for her friends." He pointed at the tree's lower branches. "There is a nest. It belongs to a pair of cardinals. Sometimes I hear them singing when I come to visit Sofia."

Rosa tried to picture Sofia. Did Uncle Sal

have any photographs of her? Maybe he'd thrown them all out after she died, the way Papa had thrown out Joseph's bassinet. Or maybe Uncle Sal had hidden the pictures from Aunt Ida.

"Does Aunt Ida know about Sofia?" It felt odd to say her name. Rosa wondered if she should have said "Aunt Sofia."

Uncle Sal nodded. "After Sofia died, I never thought I would marry again. No one could ever take her place in *mio cuore.*" He touched his hand to his heart. "When I met Ida years later, at her father's wake, she was *desolata.* Lonely, like me. Her mother had died in the Old Country, and Ida had no family here." Uncle Sal looked at Rosa. "You know, she is from my village?"

"Yes," Rosa answered. Papa had told the story many times — how unlikely it had been for Uncle Sal to find a wife in America who was from their tiny hometown. Aunt Ida had been a young girl when Uncle Sal left Italy.

Uncle Sal and Aunt Ida were so different,

Rosa had always thought he'd married her mainly because she came from his village. Aunt Ida prepared all the foods he had grown up with, and even joined in singing the village song at family get-togethers. She had a surprisingly beautiful singing voice.

"I came to love Ida," Uncle Sal went on, "but in a different way than I loved Sofia." He rubbed his hand over the top of the tombstone. "Ida does not mind that I come here. It gives me *pace.*"

Peace—that was the look in Uncle Sal's face. Rosa had thought you could only feel sad in a cemetery.

After a few minutes, Uncle Sal said, "We should visit the baby's grave now."

They went back to the car for the other flower pot. Uncle Sal carried it as he led Rosa across the road to another part of the cemetery. On the way, they passed a statue of Saint Francis holding a sparrow in his hands. The pale pink statue looked newer than Our Lady of Lourdes. In this section, fresh sod covered many of the graves, and the smell of wet dirt hung in the air.

Uncle Sal stopped in front of a large tombstone shaped like a cross. Instead of placing the pot of geraniums in front of the cross, though, he set it down in the middle of the next plot.

Rosa read the name on the cross, but it wasn't Joseph's name. She turned to Uncle Sal. "Where's Joseph's grave?"

Uncle Sal pointed at the ground beneath the flower pot. "Here."

The pot stood on a rectangular patch of bright green sod. A dirt line separated the sod from the surrounding, dull green grass. Rosa walked to the center of the plot. "Joseph is buried here?"

Uncle Sal nodded.

Rosa dropped to her knees and ran her fingers through the damp grass. This was the closest she'd ever been to her brother. She had a sudden urge to rip out the sod and dig up the holy ground with her bare hands. She longed to lay her hands on Joseph's coffin, to touch something of his. Just as Uncle Sal had touched Sofia's tombstone.

Rosa looked up at Uncle Sal. "Where's his tombstone?"

"Your father has not bought one." Uncle Sal leaned against the stone cross on the next grave. "Maybe he thinks the pain will go away faster without a monument."

Rosa shook her head. Not having a tombstone would only make the pain worse. When the sod grew into place, the line around Joseph's grave would disappear, and there would be no way to tell where he'd been buried. It would be as if Joseph had never existed.

A baby should have a small tombstone, Rosa thought, even smaller than the one on Sofia's grave. But it could be the same lovely shade of red-violet. Rosa stared at the bright green sod and pictured the tombstone in her mind. It would read:

JOSEPH PASQUALE BERNARDI
May 1, 1967 — May 1, 1967

Rosa swallowed hard and closed her eyes. She saw herself standing at the entrance to a cave. A cold mist crept out from the cave and wrapped itself around her. Rosa shivered.

"Rosa, are you all right?"

She opened her eyes. "I'm okay. Just a little wet." The dampness of the ground had seeped into her clothes, sending a chill through her whole body. Rosa stood and shook loose her clammy pants.

"We better go," Uncle Sal said. "I promised to take Ida to her father's grave today."

As they walked away, Rosa glanced back one last time. The pot of red geraniums looked so small standing alone on the unmarked grave.

On the way back to the car, Rosa asked, "Is Aunt Ida's father buried here?"

"No," Uncle Sal answered. "He is in a *camposanto* on the South Side, near their old house. Ida took care of him all by herself until the day he died. I do not think she expected to marry, especially not an old man like me." Uncle Sal winked, then turned to unlock the car.

When they were both inside, Rosa said, "Didn't Aunt Ida have any brothers or sisters?"

"She had a baby brother," Uncle Sal said, starting the engine. "But he died when she was young." Uncle Sal patted Rosa's arm. "I guess she is like you."

As they drove away, Rosa stared out her window. She tried to sort through her thoughts.

Uncle Sal had been married before.

Papa had refused to put a tombstone on baby Joseph's grave.

Aunt Ida had lost her only brother, just like Rosa.

Yet Aunt Ida had kept Rosa from going to baby Joseph's funeral. Aunt Ida, of all people, should have known what going to the funeral meant to Rosa.

Uncle Sal was wrong. Aunt Ida wasn't anything like Rosa.

20 🐝

Spelling Bee

ROSA ATE SUPPER alone that night. Papa was home for the holiday, but he was feeding Ma in her room. She had refused to come to the kitchen again.

As Rosa picked at the steak Papa had grilled, she noticed the prescription bottle sitting on the table. Ma had been taking her new medicine for almost a week now, but she didn't seem any better. More than ever, Rosa hoped that winning the bee would be the medicine that finally fixed Ma.

Rosa cleaned up quickly, then went to her room to study. She'd gone over the spelling words so many times she knew them by heart. Yet she worried that wasn't enough. So much depended on her winning.

Sitting at her desk, Rosa reached for the cross around her neck. She started to ask God to let her win the bee, then stopped. That seemed wrong. She wanted to prove that destiny didn't control everything, but she didn't know if destiny was connected to God somehow. So instead, she prayed, "Dear God, you know how hard I've studied. Please help me to remember everything tomorrow. Please help me to do my best." She made the sign of the cross, then went back to studying.

She woke the next morning still at her desk, the crumpled word list in her hand.

In the kitchen, Aunt Ida had toast and scrambled eggs ready for her. "Salvatore told me the spelling contest is today," Aunt Ida said, pouring milk into Rosa's glass. "You'll think better on a full stomach."

Rosa nodded. She didn't understand why Aunt Ida was being so nice—AnnaMaria wasn't even around.

Aunt Ida sat down with a cup of coffee. "You know, I was in a contest when I was your age. A singing contest." Aunt Ida smiled. "I came in first place, and had the honor of singing for the town festival."

Rosa took a long drink of milk. If she won the bee, that would make two things she and her godmother had in common. After what Uncle Sal had said yesterday, Rosa wondered if she was more like Aunt Ida than she'd thought. Still, Aunt Ida's new friendliness made Rosa uneasy. She finished her breakfast quickly.

On the way to school, AnnaMaria said, "I bet you'll take first place in the bee today, Rosa."

The eggs in Rosa's stomach did a flip-flop. Despite all her studying, she didn't feel very confident. "It won't be easy to beat Patrick," Rosa said. Patrick O'Shea was the best speller in their fourth-grade class, and he had been the third-grade champion the year before. "I may end up in second place."

"But *I'm* planning to come in second," AnnaMaria said with a laugh, "so you're going to *have* to win."

Rosa smiled. She really did have to win. But not for AnnaMaria.

Rosa was glad spelling came before lunch. With her queasy stomach, she wouldn't be able to eat again until the bee was over.

Sister Mary Ambrose divided the class into two groups. AnnaMaria and Rosa ended up standing on opposite sides of the room, facing each other. After explaining the rules, Sister sat down at her desk and began announcing the spelling words. Each person had to repeat the word, spell it, then say the word again.

Rosa recognized many of the words from

the year before. When Sister gave Debbie Kowalski the word *ancient,* Rosa smiled, remembering how Ma had pronounced it "ahn-chee-aint." Rosa spelled the word in her head while Debbie struggled, forgetting the *e.* Debbie seemed surprised when Sister said, "I'm sorry, Deborah. That is incorrect."

One after another, students sat down. Finally there were only four left: AnnaMaria, Patrick O'Shea, Lynn Anderson, and Rosa.

Rosa wiped her sweaty palms on the front of her jumper. She tried not to think about anything except the next word. It was AnnaMaria's turn. Her word was *indispensable,* but she spelled it wrong.

Things happened so fast after that, Rosa didn't have time to feel sorry for AnnaMaria. Patrick spelled *indispensable* without any trouble. He grinned smugly as Lynn went down on *sympathy.*

Then it was Rosa's turn again. *Sympathy* was a new word this year, but one she remembered from studying the list. She took a breath and said, *Sympathy.* S-Y-M-P-A-T-H-Y. *Sympathy.*"

"Correct," Sister Ambrose said, flashing her bright smile. "Congratulations to both of you. You have qualified for the all-school competition."

As everyone applauded, Rosa smiled, too. She would represent the class in the school bee. But she still wanted to beat Patrick.

Sister stood and said, "Now we must determine the class winner." She turned toward Patrick. "The word is *foreigner.*"

Patrick hesitated, then said, "*Foreigner.*" He paused. "F-O-R-E-G-N-E-R. *Foreigner.*"

Even before Patrick had finished, Rosa started grinning. During one of their practice sessions, AnnaMaria had made the same mistake. Rosa had laughed, saying, "How could you forget? The letter *i* is in the middle of *foreigner,* just like *I* live in the middle of a family of foreigners!"

By the time Sister asked her to spell *foreigner,* Rosa's jitters had melted away. *"For-*

eigner," Rosa said, holding her head high. "F-O-R-E-I-G-N-E-R. *Foreigner.*" The class applauded again. Finally, Rosa had to spell the word *transformation* to win, which she did without trouble. Everyone clapped and cheered.

Watching Patrick slump back to his desk, Rosa couldn't help thinking of the first day of kindergarten, when he had teased her about being strange. Remembering it now, she wanted to laugh—being born into a family of foreigners had helped her win the spelling bee.

Maybe that was the part destiny had decided: where she'd be born and into what family. Still, she wouldn't have won the spelling bee if she hadn't studied *sympathy* and the other words on the list. Rosa sat up tall in her desk. She'd proven that destiny didn't control everything. She felt suddenly hopeful that Ma would be okay after all.

At lunch, kids kept coming over to congratulate Rosa. Even kids from the other fourth-grade class. The attention surprised her. For the first time since she'd told everyone about Ma having a baby, Rosa felt like she belonged.

AnnaMaria smiled across the lunch table. "You're famous now, Rosa."

Rosa felt bad for her friend, though. "Sorry you didn't come in second like you wanted, AnnaMaria."

"Oh, that." AnnaMaria laughed and waved her hand. "I was only kidding. I didn't expect to last as long as I did. My parents are going to be really happy."

Rosa crossed her fingers and hoped Ma would be happy, too. Happy enough to go back to being her old self.

Rosa couldn't wait a minute longer to tell Ma the news. She left AnnaMaria at the corner and ran the rest of the way home.

"Ma, wait till you hear," Rosa cried, dropping her books on the kitchen table. She raced down the hall waving her blue ribbon.

Rosa stopped in Ma's doorway. She paused

to catch her breath, then said, "We had the class bee today, Ma, and I won!"

Aunt Ida marched toward Rosa from the living room, her feather duster in hand. "What is the meaning of this?" Aunt Ida pointed the duster at Rosa, practically pushing it into her face. "You should know better than to disturb your mama when she is resting."

Rosa's face went hot. All the anger she'd been keeping bottled up inside came bubbling out. "You may fool other people, Aunt Ida, but you don't fool me." Rosa shoved the duster aside. "You're a mean old witch. You never told me that Ma couldn't have any more babies. And you didn't let me go to my only brother's funeral." Rosa took a breath. "You don't really want Ma to get well. You want her to stay sick so you can be in charge and boss everybody around."

"Rosa!"

Rosa turned to see Ma standing at the foot of her bed.

"How dare you speak to your *comare* that way," Ma said. "Apologize right now."

"But, Ma," Rosa stammered, "you don't understand."

"*Now*, Rosa."

Rosa turned back to Aunt Ida, expecting her to be scowling. Instead, she looked hurt. "I'm . . ." Rosa started to say "sorry," but the word caught in her throat. On top of everything else, Aunt Ida had spoiled Rosa's plan to cheer Ma up.

"I can't," Rosa said, and ran to the kitchen. She flung her blue ribbon in the trash.

21 🌺

The Cardinal's Song

ROSA THREW HERSELF on her bed without changing clothes. All those hours of studying, for what? Not only had she failed to cheer her mother up, but now Ma was mad at her.

"Aunt Ida ruined everything!" As she said the words, though, Rosa remembered the look on Aunt Ida's face. Rosa had hurt her godmother's feelings. Even worse, she'd broken her promise to God to be extra-good.

Rosa grabbed Lamby from her headboard and hugged him close. "If only I hadn't lost my temper, Lamby." Hot tears rolled down her cheeks. "Now Ma will never get better." Rosa felt sick to her stomach. She curled up on the bed clutching Lamby to her chest and cried herself to sleep.

She dreamed she was standing in the backyard, looking down at the vegetable seedlings. Something awful had happened — the plants had shriveled up.

A bird called to her, trilling out slowly, *so-sorry, so-sorry, so-sorry*. Rosa looked up to see a bright red cardinal perched on the chain link fence.

Without warning, the bird swooped from the fence, picked up Rosa, and carried her to the cemetery. The cardinal set her down on her brother's grave. As the bird flew off, his song echoed from the surrounding tombstones. *So-sorry, so-sorry, so-sorry*.

The grass covering Joseph's grave had turned a dull shade of green, and the potted geraniums were all brown. Seeing their dead leaves, Rosa's eyes filled with tears. "I never saw him," she said out loud. "My only brother. I never even got to tell him goodbye."

One of Rosa's tears fell onto a withered geranium leaf. As she watched, the leaf turned a bright green. Then the color slowly spread throughout the plant, changing the dead geraniums into a rose bush covered with buds. One by one, the buds opened into beautiful roses—first white ones, then pink, and finally red. Their fragrance filled the air.

Rosa stared in amazement. How could one plant bear roses of three different colors?

She woke to the smell of roses.

Rosa sat up. Her head hurt from crying. She took Uncle Sal's handkerchief from her nightstand, and blew long and hard. Then she tucked the soggy handkerchief into her jumper pocket.

She was thinking about the dream when someone knocked at her door. "Can I talk to you?" Aunt Ida said.

Her godmother must have come for her

apology. Rosa wiped the crusted tears from her eyes and said, "Yes."

Keeping one hand behind her back, Aunt Ida pointed at the edge of Rosa's bed with her other hand. "Can I sit?"

Rosa nodded, moving her legs to make room.

As Aunt Ida settled herself on the bed, Rosa said, "I'm sorry."

"Never mind about that," Aunt Ida said. "I came to give you this." She took her hand from behind her back and held out Rosa's blue ribbon. "I found it in the garbage. You must have dropped it there on accident."

Rosa couldn't think of anything to say. She took the ribbon.

"I cleaned it up for you," Aunt Ida said. "I'm sure your mama will want to see it."

Rosa shook her head. "I don't think so."

"She wants to talk to you, Rosa."

"Now?"

Aunt Ida nodded.

"Is she still mad?"

"No, Rosa, she's not mad."

Rosa started to get up, but Aunt Ida stopped her.

"Before you go, I want to explain something. The reason I didn't tell you everything about your mama . . ." Aunt Ida cleared her throat. "I was trying to protect you. You have no idea how *terribile* I felt that day, giving you the bad news about the baby. I didn't want to add to your sadness. And I was afraid . . ." She looked down at her hands in her lap. "I thought you might have even more bad news soon. My own mother died giving birth to my brother, Nardo, when I was only three years old." Aunt Ida looked at Rosa. "Your mama was so sick, I was afraid you might lose her the same way."

No wonder Aunt Ida had been so worried when she first heard Ma was pregnant.

"Uncle Sal told me your brother died too," Rosa said. "Did that happen at the same time?"

"No," Aunt Ida answered. "Nardo died of pneumonia when he was four."

"Then why didn't you let me go to baby Joseph's funeral?" Rosa asked. "You should have known how much I wanted to be close to my brother. To say goodbye to him."

"I didn't know," Aunt Ida said, shaking her head. "I was so young when Mama died — I don't remember her at all. But I remember Nardo. The day of his funeral was the worst day of my life." Aunt Ida looked up at the crucifix above Rosa's bed, her eyes moist. Rosa's throat tightened to see her so sad.

"Even though it was a very long time ago, I can still see the men lowering the *cofanetto* into the cold earth." Aunt Ida shivered. "When Papa dropped the first shovelful of dirt onto the coffin, I screamed out: 'Stop! He's not dead. He can't be dead.' I tried to jump in the hole to save my brother. Someone grabbed me and carried me home still screaming. For months afterward, I had nightmares of being buried alive."

Aunt Ida turned back to Rosa. "That is why I kept you from Joseph's funeral. I didn't understand how you felt, Rosa. How much more grown-up you are than I was. I hope you will forgive me."

Rosa nodded. There was an awkward moment when neither of them said anything. Then Rosa held up her blue ribbon and said, "Thanks."

"You're welcome." The bed creaked as Aunt Ida got up. "Why don't you go show it to your mama now?"

Rosa nodded.

Aunt Ida bent down and kissed Rosa's cheek — a real kiss, not one of her pretend ones. Aunt Ida must have noticed Rosa's surprise, because she smiled and said, "No lipstick to leave a stain this time."

Rosa touched the spot where Aunt Ida's lips had pressed her cheek. Even without lipstick, the kiss had left its mark.

Rosa stood and slipped the ribbon into her jumper pocket.

In the kitchen, she said to Aunt Ida, "Can I ask you one more thing?"

"What's that?"

"The day you got Ma to eat the escarole soup, how did you do that?"

"Oh, that was easy." Aunt Ida smiled. "I told her the same thing I did a few minutes ago — that she had to get well for your sake, because you needed her. But right now I think she needs you even more. Go." Aunt Ida waved Rosa on.

Ma was sitting up in bed, waiting for Rosa.

"Aunt Ida said you wanted to talk to me."

"Yes." Ma waved Rosa over. "Did you apologize?"

Rosa nodded, moving closer to the bed. "She told me things about her I didn't know."

"She's had a hard life," Ma said. "But then, none of us has had it easy. Not even you, *cara.*" Ma looked into Rosa's eyes. "I am proud of how you won the competition today after all you've been through."

Ma's words made Rosa feel warm inside. "Want to see my ribbon?"

"Sure."

Rosa reached into her pocket, but she pulled out Uncle Sal's handkerchief by mistake. When she held out the soggy old handkerchief, an amazing thing happened — Ma laughed! How Rosa had missed her mother's laugh.

Rosa laughed, too.

Ma nodded at the handkerchief. "Is that a new kind of award?"

Rosa said, "Yeah." She pointed at Uncle Sal's initials. "S.B. stands for *Spelling Bee.*"

"You sure it doesn't stand for silly *bambina*?"

"I'm not a silly little girl, Ma," Rosa said. "Just think about it. This is a very useful prize." Rosa tried to keep a straight face as she said, "What good's a ribbon when you need to blow your nose?"

Ma laughed even harder this time. So hard, a tear slipped from her eye.

"Rosa," Ma said, her voice thick, "can I borrow your award?"

22 ✿

Roses

THE SATURDAY AFTER the spelling bee, Aunt Ida offered to teach Rosa how to bake bread. With Papa at work, Uncle Sal doing chores back home, and Ma in bed, Aunt Ida and Rosa had the kitchen to themselves.

"Here, Rosa," Aunt Ida said. "Put this on." She handed her Ma's apron. The front of the brown cloth was still streaked with flour from the last time Ma had made bread exactly five weeks earlier, on Rosa's birthday. That day seemed so long ago now.

With Ma's apron on, Rosa coated her hands with flour just the way Ma had done. Aunt Ida helped Rosa until she was kneading her own ball of dough on the wooden bread board. But the lumpy ball stuck to Rosa's fingers.

"It needs more *farina*," Aunt Ida said. She sprinkled a handful of flour onto the dough.

Rosa resumed kneading, with Aunt Ida coaching her along. "Don't be afraid to press hard. . . . Use your palms. . . . See, it's smoother now."

Rosa enjoyed the feel of the soft, supple dough in her hands.

"That's enough," Aunt Ida said finally. "If you overwork it, the bread will not rise." She covered the dough with a linen cloth. "It is good that you learn to make bread now," she said. "Your mama will need your help after Salvatore and I stop coming around."

"Are you going somewhere?"

"No," Aunt Ida said. "But your mama won't want us here much longer. She is getting stronger every day."

Rosa nodded. Ma had stayed up for two whole hours the evening before, laughing and talking like her old self. She still went to bed early, but Rosa felt her prayers for Ma to get well had finally been answered.

As she turned to wash her hands, Rosa noticed the statue of the Blessed Mother and baby Jesus on the counter, next to the fridge. The ceramic figure reminded Rosa of how she'd been unable to pray the day of Joseph's funeral.

Aunt Ida must have noticed Rosa staring at the statue. "I was praying this morning," Aunt Ida explained. She returned the statue to its usual place on the fridge. "Thanking *la Madonna* for answering my prayers for your mama."

Rosa let the water run over her hands. "I prayed for Ma, too," she said. "Just like I prayed and prayed for God to send me a baby brother." Rosa worked the dough from her sticky fingers as she spoke. "There's something I don't understand. God answered my prayers for a brother, but then He let Joseph die. Does that mean I did something wrong?"

"No, Rosa," Aunt Ida said. "But I worried the same way after my brother, Nardo, died. I prayed so hard for him to get well. When he died, I thought I didn't pray hard enough. I felt bad for a long time." Aunt Ida handed Rosa a towel. "Then, one day I asked my *nonna* about it. You know what she said to me?"

Rosa shook her head. She dried her hands as her godmother went on.

"I remember her exact words. She said, 'Idalina'—that's what she called me—'Idalina, do you *really* think God would punish you for praying?'"

Rosa had never thought of it like that. Still, she wondered. "Then why did your brother die? And why did Joseph die?"

"I don't know, Rosa." Aunt Ida sat down at the table. "Some would say it was their *destino* to die young. But I think *destino* is just something to blame for what we cannot explain." Aunt Ida shrugged. "*È un mistero.*"

A mystery. So many things about God were a mystery to Rosa.

After a moment, Aunt Ida said, "I believe with all my heart that God hears our prayers. And that when bad things happen, God finds a way to turn them to good. Papa would never have brought me to America if Mama and Nardo had lived. And I would never have met Salvatore if Papa hadn't died when he did."

Rosa had been too upset to notice before, but some good things *had* happened since baby Joseph's death. Things like planting and tending the garden with Uncle Sal; studying with AnnaMaria and winning the spelling bee; and now, learning how to make bread with Aunt Ida.

"I *am* glad you and Uncle Sal came to help us," Rosa said. She put her arm around Aunt Ida's shoulders.

"Me too," Aunt Ida said. "But I think you helped me more than I helped you."

"How?" Rosa asked.

"You let me feel needed for a while."

Rosa smiled. Uncle Sal was right after all —
she and Aunt Ida really were a lot alike. Rosa
kissed Aunt Ida's cheek. "I'll always need you,
Aunt Ida. You're my godmother."

On the last day of school, Rosa came home to
find Uncle Sal in the backyard staking the
tomato plants. Ma sat nearby in a lawn chair,
handing him strips of old rags to tie the plants
to the wooden stakes.

"Look, Rosa," Ma said. "Some of your tomatoes have flowers."

Sure enough, yellow blossoms dotted the
tomato plants. They weren't seedlings anymore. It wouldn't be long before they started
bearing fruit.

"So, Rosa," Uncle Sal said, "school is
finished?"

"Yep," Rosa answered. "I'm a fifth grader
now."

Uncle Sal stepped out of the garden and
onto the grass. "Then I should get our Cubs
tickets, to celebrate the end of the year."

"This time I'll bring my mitt," Rosa said. "Just in case another foul ball comes at us."

Uncle Sal laughed. "Good idea. You can protect me."

"Rosa," Ma said. "Today I told Uncle Sal that he and Aunt Ida don't have to come over so much anymore. With school out now, you can be my helper."

Rosa smiled. "That's right." She looked around. "Where is Aunt Ida?"

"Inside, resting," Uncle Sal said. "The heat, it makes her tired. And it makes me thirsty. I need something cold to drink. How about you, Francesca?"

"I'm fine, Uncle Sal," Ma said.

"I'll come in with you, Uncle Sal," Rosa said. "I'm thirsty, too."

In the kitchen, Rosa poured two glasses of iced tea.

After taking a long drink, Uncle Sal said, "Tomorrow, I go back to *camposanto* to put flowers on Sofia's grave. It is our *anniversario*. The anniversary of our marriage." He set his glass on the table. "Would you like to come with me?"

"Yes," Rosa said.

The next day, Uncle Sal and Rosa stopped at the florist again on their way to the cemetery. But instead of geraniums, Uncle Sal picked out a large pot of red roses. "On our wedding day, Sofia carried only one red rose," he said. "Now I can afford to give her more."

"Can I get some for Joseph, too?"

"Sure."

Rosa looked at all the potted roses — so many to choose from. She liked the pink roses best, but the white ones looked lovely, too, and the red were such a deep, rich color. Rosa just couldn't decide. Finally, she picked one of each.

"Three?" Uncle Sal said, his eyebrows raised in surprise.

"Is it okay? I got the little ones."

Uncle Sal smiled. "If that is what you want."

They drove right into the cemetery — no waiting in line today. Rosa got out of the car and looked up at the statue of Our Lady of Lourdes. Ma didn't need Our Lady's help anymore, but Papa could sure use a miracle. The strange shadow had become a permanent part of his face.

As they walked to Sofia's grave, Rosa said, "Uncle Sal, why isn't Papa happy now that Ma is better?"

"I am sure he is happy about your mama," Uncle Sal said. "But I imagine these days he is thinking more about how he lost his only son." Uncle Sal shook his head. "I pray that, in time, your papa will let go of his anger and face the pain." Uncle Sal put a hand on Rosa's shoulder. "Then he will appreciate his blessings again."

At Sofia's grave, Uncle Sal removed the pot of geraniums from the holder at the base of the tombstone and replaced it with the roses. As he knelt with his hat in his hand, Rosa heard a cardinal calling. *Purty-purty-purty-purty.* The sound came from the maple tree near Sofia's grave. Rosa thought she saw a patch of red high in the branches, but she wasn't sure.

They went back to the car for the other flowers. Rosa wanted to carry all three pots, but Uncle Sal insisted on taking one. By the time they reached the statue of Saint Francis holding the sparrow, the two little pots had grown heavy in Rosa's hands. She shifted them to her arms, cradling the plants like babies.

When they reached Joseph's grave, the pot of geraniums they had left last time lay on its side. Some of the dirt had spilled onto the ground. "Last night's storm must have knocked them over," Uncle Sal said. He set down the rose plant he'd been carrying and picked up the geraniums.

Rosa placed the other rose pots on the ground. "The same thing could happen to these," she said. In her mind, she saw the three little pots being picked up and carried away by the wind. If only Papa had given Joseph a tombstone. Then there'd be something to support the flower pots.

Rosa looked at the large, cross-shaped tombstone on the next grave and noticed the orange marigolds beneath it. The flowers weren't potted — they were planted in the soil. Rosa pointed at them. "Could we put the roses in the ground, like those marigolds?"

"I don't know, Rosa." Uncle Sal rubbed his chin. "How would we dig up the sod? I don't have a spade."

Rosa looked around the cemetery. Across the road, she spotted a family planting flowers at a grave. "We could ask to borrow theirs," Rosa said.

Uncle Sal shrugged. "Well, it cannot hurt to ask."

A few minutes later, he came back with the spade and started digging.

Before long, he'd made a large, square hole in the middle of the grave. "That should do," he said. He leaned against the spade and wiped the sweat from his forehead with his handkerchief.

"Excuse me," the man who owned the spade called from across the road. "We're leaving now. Can I have my spade?"

Uncle Sal waved. "Be right there." To Rosa he said, "I guess we'll have to finish with our hands."

While Uncle Sal returned the spade, Rosa knelt beside the hole. She dug her fingers into the loose dirt, inhaling its earthy smell. This was the closest she'd ever be to her brother. She leaned in as far as she could. "Joseph," she whispered. "It's me, Rosa. Your sister."

Rosa took the white rose, the smallest of the three plants, and turned it upside down. She patted the bottom of the pot and slipped it off, just as Uncle Sal had shown her when they planted the tomato seedlings. Then she set the rose at the front of the hole.

After un-potting the red and pink roses, Rosa placed them a little behind and to the sides of the white one, so that the three plants formed a triangle. Then she started pushing back the dug-up dirt. It felt good to fill the hole.

"Let me help you," Uncle Sal said when he returned. Together, they packed the dirt down around the roses. Then they stood to admire their work.

"*Molto bello*," Uncle Sal said.

Rosa smiled. The triangle of roses was more beautiful than any stone monument.

Uncle Sal held out his dirty hands. "Now we need to wash. Bring the flower pots. We will carry back some water for the roses."

Uncle Sal cranked the pump handle while Rosa held the empty flower pot under the faucet. "We will have to come back to take care of the roses," he said, "or they will not grow."

Rosa nodded. She liked the idea of returning to tend the flowers. Maybe Ma could come, too. And with both Uncle Sal and Rosa praying for Papa, maybe one day he would join them as well.

"We should bring some rose food next time," Uncle Sal said.

"And a watering can." Rosa held up the flower pot. Water poured out the drainage holes.

"Hurry," Uncle Sal said. "Run back before all the water gets out."

Uncle Sal and Rosa ran back and forth between the pump and the roses, carrying as much water as they could in the leaking flower pots. Rosa felt like a clown in a circus relay race.

"*Basta*," Uncle Sal said, panting. "Enough." He dropped down beside the roses. "Next time we bring the hose."

Rosa laughed as she tumbled onto the grass beside Uncle Sal. Then she quickly covered her mouth. "Uncle Sal, is it okay to laugh in a cemetery?"

"Why not?" he said. "You think the dead would not want us to be happy?"

Rosa shook her head. She couldn't imagine Joseph wanting her to feel sad.

They rested a few more minutes. Then Uncle Sal pushed himself up to a stand. "It's getting late. We better go."

Just as they reached the statue of Saint Francis, Rosa heard a cardinal calling again. *Purty-purty-purty-purty.* She stopped and listened. The song seemed to be coming from the direction of Joseph's grave. "I forgot something," she said.

Rosa ran back to her brother's grave. Between breaths she said, "Joseph. It's me again. Rosa. I forgot to tell you something."

When she was finally breathing normally again, Rosa bent down over the triangle of roses till she was close enough to smell them. *"Ciao."*

❧ *Glossary*

andiamo   let's go

anguilla   eel

anniversario   anniversary

azzurri   blue (masculine plural form)

baccalà   codfish

bambina   baby girl, little girl

bambini   young children

bambino   baby boy, little boy

bambino mio   my baby boy

basta   that's enough

bellissimo   very beautiful

bello   beautiful

biscotti   cookies

brava   well done (feminine form)

Buon appetito!   Eat up!

Buon giorno   Good morning or good day

Buon Natale   Merry Christmas

calamari   squid

camposanto   cemetery

cara   dear (feminine form)

certo   of course; certainly

ciao   hello or goodbye

cofanetto   coffin

colazione   breakfast

comare   godmother

compare   godfather

congratulazioni   congratulations

condoglianzi   condolences

coraggio   courage

desolata   desolate; sad and lonesome
   (feminine form)

destino   destiny

due   two

due mesi   two months

È nato morto   He was stillborn

erbacce weeds

espresso strong Italian coffee

È un mistero It's a mystery

Fa freddo It's cold outside

farina flour

finito finished; done

frittata omelet

furiosa furious (feminine form)

grazie thank you

impossibile impossible

incinta pregnant

la Madonna the Blessed Mother

la mia uccellina   my little bird

latte   milk

l'ospedale   the hospital

maschio   male

mesi   months

Mi dispiace   I'm sorry

mille auguri   a thousand good wishes

mille grazie   thank you very much

mio cuore   my heart

mistero   mystery

molto bello   very beautiful

Non mi lasciare   Don't leave me

Non è giusto   It isn't right; It's not fair

nonna   grandmother

nonno   grandfather

onore   honor

pace   peace

pannolino   diaper

pastina   soup made with tiny noodles

penna   pen

per devozione   for tradition's sake

Permesso?   May I come in?

persistente   persistent

Piazza San Marco   Saint Mark's Square

pizzelle   thin, waffle-like cookies

proprietà   property

salsiccie   sausages

Salute!   To your health!

scarola   escarole

scarola in brodo   escarole soup

scuola   school

sì   yes

signora   madam; Mrs.

sola   alone; lonely (feminine form)

sorpresa   surprise

straordinarie   extraordinary
  (feminine plural form)

terribile   terrible

tre   three

uccellina   little bird (feminine form)

uno   one

uno, due, tre   one, two, three

Venezia   Venice (Italy)

vieni   come

ACKNOWLEDGMENTS

I am grateful to many people for their assistance in the creation of this book. In particular, I would like to thank:

Sharon Darrow, for inspiring me to pursue an MFA in Writing for Children and Young Adults at Vermont College.

Louise Hawes, Phyllis Root, and the members of my second-semester workshop, for persuading me to expand my short story "Rosa's Prayer" into a novel.

My faculty advisors: Marion Dane Bauer, Carolyn Coman, Amy Ehrlich, and Jane Resh Thomas, for their invaluable feedback and guidance.

The Hive, an incredibly generous group of writers, for their advice, encouragement, and support.

Sister Joan Weisenbeck, FSPA, and Sister Patricia Kolas, PHJC, for encouraging me to "try to love the Questions."

My ever-patient critique group, for helping me get the details right.

Esther Hershenhorn, "a true friend and a good writer," for reassuring me that persistence is indeed rewarded.

Melissa Pankuch, my first young reader, for her insights and enthusiasm.

My editors, Cynthia Platt and Sarah Ketchersid, for asking the questions that made me dig deeper.

Danielle Capobianco, for proofreading and correcting my Italian — *mille grazie*!

My family and friends, especially Germaine Olson, Thea Sakelaris, and Sharon Wussow, for cheering me on.

And most of all, John and Thomas Martino, for putting up with me through it all.